RISING ABOVE

This is a work of fiction. Names, characters, places and incidents are either the product of the author's imagination or are used fictitiously. Any resemblance to actual persons, living or dead, business establishments, events, or locales is entirely coincidental.

ISBN: 0-9843096-5-9
ISBN-13: 978-0-9843096-5-8

www.aninkmover.com

RISING ABOVE

THE AURA OPERATION SERIES

KEVIN MORAN

ONE

Temporary Freedom

Ayla stared into the pit. It had been seconds since the Colonel was pushed in, but his screams still echoed inside the tent. Derek and the General stood with weapons in hand, holding captive the guards who'd had them a moment ago. The trio was free, but only from the immediate threat of the Colonel. Outside the tent was another horror story.

"Now we get the hell out of here, right?" Derek said.

Ayla held up a finger, walked toward the entrance, and poked her head out. She was with the last group that left Chicago, heading for the treehouse, but all the groups before hers had been ambushed. Everyone was blindsided and scattered with their captors among similar tents dotting the landscape.

She ducked back inside and ensured the tent flap was secure. "I don't think it's going to be that easy."

"How bad is it?" Derek asked.

"It may not matter," the General chimed in. "They're all Clay's men. As undisciplined as I've ever seen." He jammed his gun into the back of the guard on his knees in front of him. "They wouldn't last a minute under my watch."

"With all due respect, sir," Derek said, "I'm not sure it matters how well trained they are if they outnumber us thirty to one."

The General rubbed his fierce chin.

"Are you expecting the three of us to overpower everyone?"

"Not just us," the General said. "But maybe with the rest of the recon group who came through with us."

"They've all been separated," Ayla said. "Across the space. Tents like ours. It's hard to tell who is where."

"Doesn't seem like a good scenario," Derek added.

"I've faced worse." The General spat on the ground.

"That may be," Ayla said. "But I don't know how that helps us now. Any tactics you'd be willing to share?"

The General started pacing, his sight never leaving the guard kneeling in front of him. "Let's just think through this logically. You've been here before, right, Ayla?"

She nodded. It felt like a lifetime ago, but Thomas had brought her here to meet Lee in what she thought was going to be her escape. Not only did she end up in a worse situation, but now that she was back here, she had a hard time remembering that much about it. The previous time she was here was a bit of a blur. There were crowds and some kind of portal demonstration by Daniel, and of course, there was running. Lee was giving a speech about freedom, and she turned and ran, wanting to rescue Derek. She ran away from safety, and she was now wondering if that was where it all went wrong. Of course, without her intervening, Derek might not be with her. Without him, she wasn't sure what kind of state she'd be in. As the chaos seemed to be spiraling out of control, at least having him back in her life was keeping her relatively calm.

"Ayla?" The General's voice broke through her daydream. Her mind cleared and her attention turned to the General's gaze. "Do you remember how you got in or out in the first place?"

"Didn't we cover this before recon?"

"Briefly, but it would be really helpful to review now that we're here."

"I left through the treehouse," she said. "Just like how we came in."

"Unfortunately, that won't help us now," the General said. "There's just no way we'll make it there undetected."

"We could try," Derek said.

"Wait," Ayla added. "When I first got here, to this place, it wasn't in the treehouse." She gulped, remembering meeting with Thomas and planning an escape to this room. He'd said it would solve all of her problems, but she wasn't so sure now. It surely didn't solve his; the last time she saw Thomas, he had just been shot by Clay and his men. She felt a tug at her eyelids and pondered what happened to him. She shook it off and remembered the task at hand. "Thomas . . . he brought me through an old door."

"An old door?" Derek repeated.

"Just across from the treehouse. It was like the outside of the room, I guess. There was a tunnel we had followed for a long time. We had come from the library." The memory of finding this room for the first time, blades of grass cutting through her thin hospital shoes, flooded her brain with memories of running through her backyard and forgetting about all of life's problems. It had briefly taken her back home, only to come crashing down all around her.

Derek interrupted her memory. “Can you find it again?”

She shrugged. “Maybe. But I don’t think it’s close by. We might have to fight our way there.”

The General stopped pacing. “I think we’re going to have to try.” He slammed the butt of his weapon into the guard, who crumpled. “Can’t have them knowing our plans, though.” He nodded to Derek, who did the same, and the second guard slumped to the ground, splashing mud onto Derek’s ankles.

TWO

Old Friends

Katherine's eyes widened. "What do you mean we stepped into a trap?"

"It seems that us coming back was Clay's plan all along," Lee said.

It was all for nothing: roping Ayla into sneaking around Chicago to steal the orb, abandoning the recon group at the treehouse, coming to rescue Thomas in the hospital. Katherine sighed, exasperated by the fact that Clay had appeared to have outmaneuvered everyone again. She couldn't believe her luck, and she started to second-guess if it was worth helping Lee in the first place.

"What does that mean?" she asked.

"Clay and his men were waiting for us at the treehouse. For everyone. The General, his troops, Derek and Ayla . . ." Lee sighed. "It seems as though he's been working with the Colonel this whole time."

Betrayal had found Katherine once again. The Colonel, the General's right-hand man in Chicago, had betrayed them, just as Jeffrey had betrayed her back in Kansas City.

Of course, she thought. *Just my luck.*

She started pacing in the hallway.

"That was Clay?" Katherine's head was spinning. "So Ayla? And Derek . . ."

Lee shook his head.

This can't be right, she thought. How could Clay be communicating with the Colonel? How did the General not know? How had she let herself fall into this situation? So many questions rushed through her head and she felt dizzy.

"What . . . What does that mean . . . for us?" she eked out.

"Well, in the good news department, I'm not sure he planned for us to escape from the treehouse." Lee forced a crooked smile. "Or find Thomas."

At that moment, as if on cue, Thomas slid into the room, scraps of clothes hanging off his bony shoulders and crooked spine. His half-smile matched that on Lee's face. Katherine ran over and grabbed his frail wrist. "Let me help you," she said.

He jerked his hand away. "I'm okay. Really . . ."

"I don't think you are—"

"Well, what am I supposed to do about it?" His surprisingly loud voice erupted into the empty hallway. The trio stared at each other while the echoes died down. Thomas finally spoke up again. "Look, I'm exhausted and I don't even know what reality is anymore . . ."

"It's okay." Lee placed his arm around Thomas's protruding shoulder. Thomas quickly shrugged it off, and Lee looked at him quizzically.

"Sorry," Thomas said. "It's just been a long, excruciating series of events. Punishment and torture and confusion and I don't know who or what to trust anymore."

"I totally understand," Katherine said. Thomas's sunken eyes emanated peace, as if he had already accepted the inevitable outcome if this path had continued and Katherine and Lee hadn't shown up. The corners of his mouth went up slightly and Katherine gave him a hug. "And as painful as it might be," she kept pressing, keeping the urgency of the situation at the forefront of everyone's thoughts, "we need to figure out how to get out of here."

"What about everyone else back at the treehouse?" Lee asked. "Ayla, Derek, the General."

Katherine glanced at him. "I thought you said they were trapped?"

"And I thought Thomas was dead, but here we are." He gestured toward the frail man stooped next to him.

"Are you saying we should go back and rescue them?" Katherine asked.

"Are you saying we shouldn't?" Lee asked.

"No." Katherine was clear. "We can't take any more risk—"

"More risk?" Thomas piped in. "How is that possible? I have been days away from death for a while now. If we don't go back and at least *try* to find them, how are we better than Clay, leaving them for dead?"

Katherine sighed. After she'd been stabbed in the back by Jeffrey and cornered again by Clay, her empathy meter had started turning inward. She broke the silence with the only word that made sense in the moment. "Understood," she said. She *did* understand, although internally, she was struggling with the reasoning. "What are you suggesting we do, then?" She turned to Thomas, who seemed to have all of the answers.

"I haven't been outside of this wing lately, but you came through the central square, right?"

Lee and Katherine nodded in unison.

"What'd it look like? Any survivors?"

Lee gulped. "None that we found."

"Shit." Thomas kicked gingerly at the ground. "Clay and his men shuttled everyone to the lower levels, but I was hoping there had been some kind of uprising or recovery or . . . something . . ."

"Did he just abandon the upper levels?" Katherine asked.

"All but the hospital, and he mostly used it to keep people barely alive . . ." He choked up but continued his thought. "For some twisted reason or another."

Katherine didn't like the sound of her hospital being used for nefarious purposes, but there was little she could do about it now. "Is there anyone else here?"

"I don't know. They don't let me out of my room."

"Well, maybe we can look for help?"

Thomas glanced nervously at the clock. "Not right now," he said. "They patrol this area more heavily than others."

"So what do we do?"

"I think we have to get far away from here," Thomas said.

"Where else can we go?" Lee asked, clearly desperate to have some sort of plan come together.

"I think you know where we have to go." Thomas nodded to Lee.

"No . . ." was all Lee said. "You *just* said that's where everyone was sent to. Why would we go toward the chaos?"

"There's nothing up here that can help us anymore. The treehouse is gone, the central square is gone, the upper offices and rooms are nearly gone." Thomas looked downward and sighed. "We *have* to," he finally said.

Lee pressed on. "But we'll be walking into the line of fire."

"We have to walk somewhere."

"What are you talking about?" Katherine interrupted. In unison, Thomas and Lee broke eye contact and turned toward Katherine. It was the kind of discomfort she had only ever felt once before, when they all discovered an outsider, Ayla, had infiltrated their facility and they were trying to determine what to do. Something about the wide-eyed Lee and the near-death Thomas turning toward her sent shivers throughout her body.

Lee gulped. "We have to go to the lower levels. We might have an ally down there."

"An ally?" Katherine asked.

"Yep," Lee said. "He's actually been helping our group from the very beginning." His beard bobbed up and down with his smile. "But he doesn't particularly like to get involved directly. Like he didn't come to the treehouse to escape with us but still saw the good in our cause."

Katherine knew nearly everyone in the lower levels. She practically knew everyone in the entire facility. If she had to pick out someone to be on Lee's side the entire time, rebelling against it all, she didn't have the slightest idea who she would choose.

Addressing the blank stare on her face, Lee said, "Mr. Fixer." He said it so casually, as if it wasn't a huge surprise.

Katherine's jaw must have instinctively dropped, because Lee asked her if she was all right. "I'm . . . I'm fine," she squeaked out.

"I just don't understand . . ." She dropped her gaze to the floor, hoping to find an explanation in the recesses of her brain.

"He's been helping us plant portals, steal technology . . ." Thomas said. "He wanted to help, but he didn't want it to be obvious to anyone. Given he mostly works alone anyway, it was a win-win."

"But . . . how?" Katherine asked. Mr. Fixer was the guy who could fix things, obviously. Katherine had gone to him many times, most recently to identify what Ayla was keeping in her backpack, which turned out to be an old ID card, a camera, and a weird black rectangle. Katherine had assumed it was spy gear Ayla was using against them. She never did figure out all the secrets the gear held, but she at least knew Ayla wasn't a spy.

"He's trusted by everyone, right?" Lee said. "Who would suspect him?"

"But why help you and your group?" Katherine squinted at Lee.

"I was able to convince him." Lee shrugged. "I guess you'll have to ask him yourself."

Katherine looked suspiciously across the faces of both men. She had plenty of dealings with Mr. Fixer, but this didn't seem to be his way of operating. He had never once, in the many years he had been around, raised any sort of suspicion from Katherine or her team.

Did Raymond know about this?

Technically, Mr. Fixer reported up through Raymond as the head of operations, so surely he would have to know, right? If that was the case, why didn't Raymond help find Ayla before Clay? Why did he vote to turn Ayla over to her in the first place? Maybe he wasn't in the know? Many questions scrambled her thoughts.

"You really think he can help us?" Katherine finally asked.

"I don't know who else can," Thomas said.

Lee shrugged. "Or if we have any other options."

"How do we get to him?"

The men looked at each other again.

"Stop it," Katherine said out loud, even though she wanted to only say it internally.

Thomas glanced at the clock again. "I hate to put a damper on the party, but can we get going? I think they'll be around for checks soon."

"If they find you gone . . ." Katherine couldn't finish the sentence.

"I think I have to go back," Thomas said. "And pretend like nothing happened."

"No." Lee reached out. "I almost lost you once. I'm not prepared to do that again."

Thomas squared up to Lee. "We don't have a choice. We need to get past these guards one more time, and then I promise, we will get out of here."

"That's what they said before and look what happened. You ended up shot and tortured and I ended up back here all over again. I can't do that."

"You *have* to," Thomas insisted.

Lee raised his voice. "I can't."

"Listen to me," Thomas said. "If you don't, all of our lives are at risk. Do you understand?"

Off in the distance, the doors of the main entrance squeaked and a few nearby lights flickered to life. "Go," Thomas said. "Go, I'll be fine." He hobbled to his hospital bed, and Katherine grabbed Lee's elbow.

"He'll be okay," she assured Lee, dragging him to her old office.

A faint tear rolled down Lee's large nose until he wiped it away and ran side by side with Katherine.

* * *

Katherine's office hadn't seen visitors in a long time. Cobwebs ran from the bookshelf in the corner all the way to the makeshift couch. Dust piled an inch high on her desk. The overhead light no longer worked, but the small desk lamp flickered to life as she dragged Lee inside. She took a seat on the still-wobbly chair, and Lee plopped down on the couch, sending a cloud of dirt and debris into the small space. He took out the orb he had stored in his pocket and set it down on the makeshift milk-carton end table.

"Why didn't you tell me about Mr. Fixer?" Katherine addressed the issue before the door had even closed.

"I had an obligation to those forty-six people who joined my group." Lee coughed. "Based on everything we saw previously with my predecessor, and Clay, they still chose to follow me. I had to play it safe." He waved his arms around in the dirt-filled air. "I couldn't just go about spilling my guts to anyone I considered a friend."

"Are you saying we're not friends?" Katherine crossed her arms and kicked her foot over her leg.

"Of course we're friends, but even if one extra person knew who didn't *need* to know, the entire plan could have been at risk."

"But if I *did* know, I could have helped."

"That's easy to say now, Katherine, but I don't think that was so true back then." He let out a small laugh. "Do you even remember back then? I was a wide-eyed dreamer, and you were a rule follower. Someone who wouldn't take risks. I just couldn't risk it." He picked up the orb and tossed it back and forth. "Besides, there's nothing I can do about it now anyway."

"You're right," Katherine admitted. "We have to move on."

So many questions continued running through Katherine's head, but the answers wouldn't make a difference now. She was used to having as much information as she wanted—or needed. Sitting in her old office, once a place of knowledge and power, now felt like one of the first times in her life when she didn't know what was going on and didn't have all the information. A shiver ran up and down her arms. Goosebumps sprang up out of nowhere. Before any of this, she was in control and knew what was going on. Having a plan had been her comfort, but now, ever since Ayla had interfered with everything, the plan had been exchanged for chaos.

Her attention was drawn to Lee, who had made his way over to the desk lamp and switched it off, sending the room into darkness. The only light available was the thin stream coming from between Katherine's door and the run-down linoleum flooring.

"What are you doing?" she asked quietly, for no particular reason.

"I need to concentrate."

"On what?"

"On finding Mr. Fixer."

Another source of light appeared from the orb in Lee's hand. It was an eerie blue-green glow, and it sent Lee's shadow dancing across the room as he made his way back to the couch. He sat again, and the soft, mist-like shadows of the debris thrown from the cushions scattered on the backdrop of the wall. Lee rubbed his bald head before raising his long finger to his lips. "Shhh . . ." He clasped the ball between both hands. The light dimmed, and Lee sucked in a deep breath. The ball became even brighter, and Katherine swore Lee started vibrating. Little movements at first turned into sways on the couch, like he was sitting in a rowboat in the middle of a tumultuous ocean. The orb pulsated in his hands, sending the occasional streak of light into Katherine's eyes, who shielded them as best she could. At one point, the orb became cloudy, and an expression of concern crossed Lee's face, but before long, the cloudiness dissipated and Lee's rocking settled, and then the orb fell silent and Lee opened his eyes.

Lee snapped his head back and dropped the orb, which rolled away under the makeshift couch. His hand shot up to his head and he winced in pain. Katherine dropped to her knees and reached under the couch. She pulled the orb back to her lap, along with piles of dust and dirt. Lee muttered and groaned before slowly opening his eyes.

"He's in his workspace. We can get to him."

"How do you know that?"

"I can't describe it to you; it's something you have to experience."

"Can I try it?" she asked gleefully.

Lee snatched the orb from Katherine. "No," he said. "I mean, not now. We don't have time. Plus, it takes practice and we don't know the long-term effects yet." He shoved the orb back into his pocket, slapped his knee, and stood up. "Do you think those guards are still roaming around Thomas's room?"

"If the hospital security system is still up and running, we could check."

"How do we do that?" Lee asked.

* * *

The old, wooden door squeaked as Katherine inched it open.

Stupid old technology, she thought.

She stuck her head out, confirmed the coast was clear, and then crept down the hallway toward the main nursing station not far from her office. Lee followed her on his tiptoes, carefully shutting the door behind him. There were no odd sounds or sights in the hall, and when the door to the nurses' office finally came into view, she picked up her pace until she was able to reach the keycard slot. She casually slid hers by the reader, and the door slid upward into the wall. She and Lee continued into the room as the squeak-free door closed behind them.

"What are we looking for?" Lee whispered.

"This." Katherine stepped up to a monitor embedded in a desk in the middle of the room. It had been a while since she had to run the hospital security cameras, but standing in front of the board again jogged her memory. She metaphorically crossed her fingers as she slid her keycard into a jar of goo and jammed familiar-looking buttons on the panel. A few screens came to life, showing the hallway area of the hospital. The halls were mostly empty, with an occasional tipped-over cart, an empty bag, or strewn-about bedsheets from who knew where. A wave of nausea hit Katherine, and a chill ran through her. It felt like she was out of place, in an unfamiliar world, even though she knew every square inch of the area. The monitor finally changed to a view that looked even more familiar; it was Thomas's room. He was in bed, eyes closed, most likely not asleep.

The screen changed again. It showed the hallway outside his room. Two guards strode with purpose into the distance, steps in sync and guns by their sides. In all of Katherine's years in the hospital, there were few times she had seen guards and guns here, and sadly, all of them involved Clay somehow. Armed men in the halls always meant suffering. More suffering than was normal in the hospital. But suffering that was completely unnecessary. She resisted the urge to yell and scream and hit things. Instead, she stuffed it inside, pleasing her logical half and further suppressing her emotional half.

"Do you think they'll be gone soon?" Lee asked, startling Katherine back to reality.

"Let's wait for them to head to the exit."

"These cameras can't see outside to the central square, right?"

"I wish . . ." When Katherine was in control, she had an opportunity to push for additional surveillance capabilities, but it was a little too late for that. The cameras changed again. The two guards rounded the corner and headed for the main hallway. When they were halfway to the double-wide door that led to the central square, Katherine jumped up.

"Let's go," she said.

They bolted for the exit, but before they had taken more than a few steps, the door swung open. Standing in the frame was a familiar face. It stopped Katherine in her steps, and Lee gasped. Two guards just outside of the door stood with their guns pointed directly at Katherine and Lee, and in the middle, between the intimidating men, was a cigarette-swirling, now mustache-less bald man stepping toward them.

“Katherine, Lee.” He nodded, looking both of them over. “It’s good to see you again,” Jeffrey said.

THREE

Chicago Conflict

Ellen's attention was piqued by the sound of Ms. Ware's flats clicking against the smooth surface. Ms. Ware did not seem like a woman to chase, yet here they were, in the hallway just outside of Ellen's quarters. Less than ten minutes had passed since the guard broke the portal to Chicago, leaving Ms. Ware and her vicious, swinging bangs to freely hijack the facility and chase after the woman who had helped her do it.

"Ellen." Ms. Ware took a step forward. "I'm sorry our time in Room A was so abrupt and . . . perhaps a little rough."

Ellen chortled. It was only rough because Ms. Ware made it that way. She didn't *have to* take control of the facility in such a pushy way.

"And I take back what I said earlier; I *do* need you for something."

There it is, Ellen thought. The ask. The reason Ms. Ware had followed Ellen back to her room. *There's always a catch.*

Ellen crossed her arms. “And what exactly would that be?”

“I need you for the future, the future of these facilities.”

“Seems like you had that planned out already.”

“I do.”

Ellen was taken aback by the reply.

“But your cooperation will make it proceed much more smoothly.” Ms. Ware took another step forward. “And perhaps,” she continued, “buy you favor within our inner circle.”

Ellen raised an eyebrow.

“I know the last time you spoke with Clay wasn’t exactly friendly.”

That was a nice way to put firing a weapon at your previous boss, Ellen thought.

“But lucky for you, I have Clay’s attention—and am on his good side.”

Ellen knew Clay as well as anybody, and nobody was on his good side.

“If you help me—or, rather, help *us*—I can do some convincing.”

The doubt continued to grow, but Ellen wasn’t going to shut down the conversation prematurely; after all, her options had been dwindling for quite some time.

“Clay’s plan,” Ms. Ware continued, “includes commanders for each facility gathering and hijacking operations.”

“Commanders?” Ellen wasn’t familiar with the position in the facilities and what role these so-called commanders played.

“Clay can’t be everywhere at once,” Ms. Ware said. “Although the portals helped.” She smiled. A shiver ran down Ellen’s spine. “So he has help from others.”

“Like you?” Ellen snapped. “Or that Colonel guy?”

Ms. Ware just nodded.

Ellen wasn't sure why she'd asked; she didn't really care. "So what does all this have to do with me?"

"Your team helped build the orbs, correct?"

It was a project Ellen was all too familiar with. Her team had spent years trying to perfect teleportation, and when they thought they'd achieved it, another, experimental branch was formed to determine how far they could push the technology. After years of research and work, they discovered that the underlying technology could be torn away from the strawberry-goo portals, and they found that just about any old container would work, with some additional restrictions. Physical matter couldn't pass this way, for example. After concluding some less-than-moral experiments, they found that the orbs' best purpose was to transmit thoughts—or, rather, brain activity. In fact, the information could manifest in some ways, but the limits were reached with physical matter.

Ellen often wondered if they were dabbling outside of protocol and more into communication devices rather than transportation, but as long as the bosses were happy, she afforded herself and her teams some wiggle room. While they were still working to crack the code of two-way portals, the team tasked with orbs was making great progress on the device. It wasn't perfect and still had a long way to go.

Ellen wasn't entirely sure how Ms. Ware knew about the research, but here she was, standing, waiting for an answer.

"My team *did* build them, yes."

"We need you to make them better."

"Impossible." Ellen shook her head. "Everything for that

entirely experimental research," she emphasized, "is back in Kansas City, which, as of ten minutes ago, I don't have access to." The corners of Ellen's mouth curled upward, and she forced them back down.

Ms. Ware waved her hand. "Don't worry about that. Assume everything you need is already here."

Ellen closed her eyes. She had worked with the team here. They were well below her standards. Not to mention, the supplies and materials she had access to were severely lacking. Ms. Ware was lying, but she wasn't sure why yet.

"If you had everything, how long would it take you to fine-tune it?" Ms. Ware continued.

Ellen squinted at Ms. Ware, who was staring out the window to the open floor below. The direction of this conversation was murky, and Ellen wanted to make sure she wasn't steering it the wrong way. Nine out of ten times, she wouldn't even consider helping Ms. Ware, and her immediate response would be to blow her off, but in this case, the tables were turned and she had to analyze the details a bit more closely.

"Why do you ask?" Ellen stalled.

"We need to coordinate moves between the facilities. There is currently no great method to do that." Ms. Ware's gaze turned from the floor back to Ellen. "We can communicate within a facility, sure; that's easy. But between them, there are just too many challenges. Your orbs solve this problem."

Ellen shrugged. "They won't help. They're entirely passive." She paused. That was mostly true outside of a few experiments, not that Ms. Ware would understand the details or, necessarily, care about them. "Maybe," she continued. "And I mean in theory only. Maybe they could be used that way, like long-distance walkie-talkies, I suppose, but they are explicitly not designed for it."

"That's why I'm asking." Ms. Ware sighed. "Can it be done? Can *you* do it?"

Ellen saw two possibilities. She could refuse and outright tell Ms. Ware it couldn't be done, or she could fully cooperate, knowing full well a technical design change like the one she was asking for was, at the very least, half a year off. She had to steer herself back into a position with leverage. If she worked with Ms. Ware and the team here, she'd have leverage, regardless of how small. They'd have to at least give her a chance. If she denied the request, there was no telling what would happen to her. She imagined something like the pit . . . or worse.

"It could be done, yes, but—"

"That's all I need to know for now."

"The logistics alone are mind-boggling," Ellen continued, needing to finish her thought.

"Let me worry about the logistics."

"I don't have a time frame."

"You have two days."

Ellen's eyes nearly popped out of their sockets. "Two days?"

"Is that going to be a problem?"

Yes!

Of course!

That's impossible!

Ellen wanted to scream, and the urge to wrangle Ms. Ware to the ground and crush her windpipe nearly overcame her earlier analysis; leverage was better. She clenched her fists and ground her teeth. She paused and counted to three, suppressing her instincts. After collecting her thoughts, she relaxed her fists and jaw muscles and gulped. “I’ll see what I can do.”

FOUR

Commandeer

Audible gasps rang out through the boardroom when Steven entered with Clay, and Richard was nowhere to be seen. Whispers circled throughout the group, the members of which were seated at the round table in the middle of the room, cloaked in dark wood and tapestries. Steven headed straight for his usual chair, but Clay skulked behind deliberately and carefully walked around each person at the table. His breath was heavy, his gaze never left the group members, and the whispers died down as he circled around each member before making his way to his own seat—or, rather, Richard's seat. The chair made a muffled noise as Clay backed it away from the table, rolling against the heavy, red carpet. Clay sat, moved closer to the table, and directed his gaze at the ceiling. The tension was building as the whispers died down into inescapable silence. Clay lowered his head and scanned each member of the group one last time before speaking.

"Nice to finally meet everyone in person." He forced a smile across his face. "I'm Clay, but you probably already knew that." His smile transformed into a smirk as his statement hung in the air.

Paul Leveer, the representative from Kansas City, leaned forward in his chair. "Where's Richard?"

Clay picked up the short glass in front of him, which contained Richard's favorite rum. He finished the entire thing and, still holding the glass, smoothed out the tablecloth in front of him. Steven writhed in his chair and grasped at his tie to loosen it. He had just witnessed his boss murdered in cold blood by the very man that now sat next to him, drinking the deceased's favorite rum as if nothing had happened. Steven stared into Clay's cold blue eyes and, for the first time, realized what it was like to see a man with no soul.

Clay finally addressed Paul. "Richard won't be able to make it tonight."

"Why not?" Paul was quick to respond. The rest of the group let him.

"Or any night, for that matter." Clay ignored Paul's question. "I'm running this group now." Clay slammed the glass into the smooth tablecloth, sending a loud thud through the room. The table shook and ice clanked in the other drinks.

"What'd you do to him?" Rufus, the New York representative, jumped into the discussion. He was the oldest member of the group. His eyes sank into his face, and his bones protruded from his cheeks. He looked as if he could pass away at any minute. His voice was soft, and Steven wasn't even sure he had heard him talk before. To be fair, almost no one in the group spoke when Richard was around; he drove every conversation and shut down questions quickly. Unfortunately, Steven felt like Clay was going to run these meetings the same way, if not in a fiercer and more controlling manner.

"How are you still alive?" Clay laughed. "A strong wind could take you out." He winked, and Rufus slunk back in his chair.

"Did you kill Richard?" Alex Carey, from Chicago, asked. Alex was more spry than Rufus, but it was all very relative. He was still older than Steven, Clay, and likely even Richard. Before joining this operation, Steven always joked about how old guys were running everything, but he had been living the joke for years now.

"Don't worry about what I did or didn't do—"

"You murdered him, you son of a bitch." Paul interrupted Clay and stood. His scrawny, accusatory finger hung in the air, pointing at the man across the table. "You can't do that."

Clay stood, flinging his chair backward and tipping it over. "I can do whatever the hell I want," he said firmly. "I'm in charge and nobody can stop me." His blue eyes pierced everyone else at the table. "Least of all this group of frail old men." He scowled. "Now sit down!"

"And if I don't?" Paul defied Clay's demands.

Clay slapped his empty rum glass across the room. It shattered against the oak wainscotting and sent shards crashing into the wall. Paul didn't flinch. "You don't have a choice," Clay commanded. "You had a choice when Richard was here, but seeing as how you"—he paused and looked around the table—"how you *all* didn't give a shit about how he ran things and said nothing while the facilities were burning, then you certainly don't have a say now. You were all too scared to stand up to Richard and how he ran things." Clay leaned against the table, clenching his hands into fists. "I'm certainly no Richard, and I sure as shit aren't going to have you interfere with the plan I've got in place now. So if you *don't* sit down," he said, glaring at Paul, "then we're going to have a problem." He paused. His nostrils flared as he let the men digest his words. Steven knew by now that this was mostly a move of dominance and some dramatic effect. "Do you want a problem?"

Paul broke eye contact and pleaded with the rest of the men. "We can't have this maniac running the show. He'll expose us all! We've worked too hard to have—"

Clay lunged for Paul's throat, wrapping his hands tightly around his windpipe. "Hm, hm, good points, good points," Clay muttered through gritted teeth. Paul grasped at Clay's hands, his face slowly turning red. "But you know what? I'm tired of you already." With one hand wrapped around his throat, Clay moved his other to grab Paul's chin. He guided Paul's head to look around the table, like a human puppet. "What do you say, group? Are you going to listen to this guy? Do you like his ideas?" The veins in Clay's neck protruded outward, and his eyes were wide and bloodshot, like a man on an all-week bender. "Or do you think it's just a good idea to shut up and listen to Clay?" Clay threw Paul back into his chair, picked up the half-full glass at his seat, and threw it at Paul's head. Blood and booze rushed down Paul's forehead as he collapsed in his chair, grasping at his wound.

The room fell silent. Sweat darkened the other men's suits as they held their breath, afraid to even breathe. Steven wasn't even sure there were words to be said. What could be said after such a display of force? Richard, in a million years, would have never done such a thing, but their new leader stood crooked like a madman, staring at the damage he had done to Paul. His eyes eventually veered to the men, each still holding his breath, before his gaze finally landed on Steven. Steven blinked slowly, hoping it was just a dream but knowing full well it was his new reality.

"Let's go," Clay said, adjusting his jacket and walking toward the portal.

Steven inched his chair backward, nodding at the men around the table, fully acknowledging the crazy situation.

On their way out, Clay shouted back at the group, "If you have any questions, don't ask them. We'll meet again."

FIVE

Trap and Rescue

"Jeffrey . . ." Katherine didn't know what to say.

"You look surprised." Jeffrey took another step forward.

"Are you working for Clay now?" Lee asked.

Jeffrey held up his hand and Lee stopped. The guards who had been standing in the hallway marched forward, following Jeffrey into the room. Jeffrey took a long drag on his cigarette, and the smoke wafted around the now-cramped space. "Somehow I always knew you two would be back," he said.

"What have you done here?" Katherine had to restrain herself from yelling in his face. It helped that Lee's hand was gently holding her back.

Jeffrey smiled. "We did what we had to do. We simply made sure that the little mistake we made with you two . . . and the others . . ." He flicked ashes off the end of his dwindling cigarette. "That *that* mistake was closed."

"You mean the mistake of letting us escape?" Lee asked.

"Precisely. It's not something the facility could afford."

"But the damage to the central square, the hospital, our own place . . ." Lee's hand pressed harder against Katherine's shoulder. It was for the best; Katherine could feel herself losing control, a feeling she didn't have much experience with. She had never wanted to strangle anyone before, let alone her own prior colleague, but with Jeffrey's scrawny neck sticking out like a toothpick, she couldn't shake the thought.

"It's not the facility you once knew, but don't be mistaken: there's plenty still going on here," Jeffrey said.

"What does that mean?" Katherine blurted.

"When you suddenly departed, Clay was . . ." Jeffrey twirled his cigarette in the air, trying to think of an appropriate word. "Let's just say he was less than thrilled. He immediately swooped through the facility, bringing in his troops and clearing out defectors, unwanted, and rounding up, quite frankly, whomever he came across that didn't see eye to eye with him."

"So just like fifteen years ago?" Lee asked.

Jeffrey laughed. "If you thought that was bad, this was significantly worse."

Katherine audibly gasped. She couldn't imagine what worse would look like. "The incident," as it was referred to, was Clay's last foray into the facility, and all she remembered was the horribleness of it all. Families rounded up, shuffled about, questioned, abused, and isolated, all in the name of finding the rebel group, which she now knew was Lee. The irony was that Lee had escaped the first search, only to successfully lead another rebellion. Katherine had been the benefactor of the incident, being promoted to a new, highly visible position because her prior boss had been outed. However, in her mind, the outcome wasn't worth all the suffering, and if she could go back in time, she liked to think that she would have handled it differently. It had taken her a long time to cope with the events of the incident, and it seemed like just recently she had recovered from the scars. Hearing that it was happening again seemed like a horrible version of déjà vu.

"And," Jeffrey continued, "given my recent display of loyalty, I was one of the select few that Clay could actually trust and work with. Clay's new 'tactics,'"—Jeffrey air-quoted as he talked, cigarette dangling precariously between his fingers—"provided an increase of injured patients needing to receive care. I, of course, was the obvious candidate to lead those efforts, among other things. Unfortunately, with a limited staff, an increased need for information, and other circumstances, we had to make do. We lost quite a few, as you can see."

Katherine hadn't seen who else was in the hospital, if anyone at all, and she shuddered thinking about the care they received. Although she recognized that she and Jeffrey weren't exactly in the same field, they were peers, and she would have to consider what he must have done as a dereliction of duty. So much for the processes he clung to so dearly in the past, unless the processes had changed with Clay in charge. It was the only reasonable way to explain Jeffrey's behavior; she had known him for nearly her entire life, and it just didn't make sense to her.

Jeffrey rambled on. "The others were put to work, increasing output nearly tenfold, and the limited resources in Ellen's old department, once cleared of wrongdoing, were essentially chained to their desks to ramp up production."

"So it's become a facility of slaves?" Katherine asked.

Jeffrey took another small step forward, his old loafers sliding across the flooring. Katherine could smell his cigarette breath, and the stain on his teeth was more apparent than before. "Except this time," he said, "everyone knows it." His yellow teeth smiled. "I think Clay would like to see you two again."

The guards encircled Katherine and Lee with handcuffs extended. Katherine squirmed and put up a fight, but it was a waste of precious energy. She had fought and lost this battle before and wasn't looking to make anyone more pissed off than they already were. Lee struggled a bit more, and Katherine imagined it was because he likely knew it meant he wouldn't get to see Thomas again. And as if on cue, Thomas's voice called out from the hallway.

"Hey," he said. "The guards passed and I wasn't sure—" He stepped into view. Katherine's guard turned and quickly drew his gun. Thomas's hands flew up in the air.

"Thomas!" Jeffrey yelled. His voice slowly transformed into a laugh as his head swiveled between Thomas and Katherine. "So you two already knew about each other? Let me guess." His gaze focused on Lee. "You were here to save him?"

Lee looked down at the ground.

"Another thoughtless attempt, Lee?" Jeffrey laughed again. "And to think people looked up to you. Do you really plan anything or just have hope that everything will work out?" He stepped toward Lee. "You know what they say about hope, right?"

"Hey!" Thomas called out.

Jeffrey threw his cigarette on the dirty linoleum and crushed it with the sole of his freshly shined shoe. "Let's go," he said to the guards.

Katherine stumbled forward as the guard yanked her handcuffs.

* * *

Being forcefully escorted out of the room, Katherine could only shrink her shoulders and drag her feet. There was no use in fighting it anymore. Every time they had run up against something, it ended up backfiring or getting people hurt. She was stuck in an infinite loop where she thought the end was in sight, only to find out the situation would just repeat itself, and she'd be stuck in the situation until she died.

Hope broken by defeat.

Her spirit broken by no hope.

A continuous cycle of never-ending battles she was always on the wrong side of.

She slouched further and sighed as the guard in front of her dragged her toward likely pain and torture. While her reason for coming back was sound, to rescue the others still stuck here, she had started to regret her decision. She had a hard time reconciling self-preservation with the preservation of others. It was odd for her to be on the side of selfishness, but being burned so many times would do that to a person. She knew this was true, because she had treated people like this when she ran the medical facilities here.

People who had fallen in life and just couldn't get up. People who were once well-regarded workers in the facility, who maybe got let go for whatever reason and ended up peddling garbage in the central square with other vendors. It wasn't that they were somehow less of a person; it was just that they were stuck, forever, in a cycle they wished they could have avoided, but life circumstances got in the way.

Without warning, the guard in front of her crumpled like a wet biscuit. Lee's guard did the same, collapsing on his fallen friend, and Jeffrey fell to the ground. A man's work boot appeared from the hallway, stepping on top of the fallen guards. His boot led his overall-covered torso into view.

"Mr. Fixer?" Katherine asked. She realized at that point she didn't know his real name.

"Andrew," his low, growly voice said. Katherine took his extended, calloused hand. His bulging muscular form carried her with ease over the fallen guards and into a clearing in the hallway. Jeffrey was sitting cross-legged on the floor, already having been bound and gagged. Standing above him was another familiar, freshly dressed face.

A slight smile ran across Katherine's face. "Raymond," she said.

"Good to see you." He stepped forward with a small key and unlocked her cuffs. Typically, he was dressed immaculately and was well put together, but his hair was unusually disheveled, and he had missed a button on the shirt underneath his grease-stained suit jacket. The man who, at least once, ran infrastructure and operations seemed as though he had been through a lot recently. He stepped behind Katherine and over to Lee to unlock his handcuffs, and Lee immediately ran over to Thomas.

"What . . . What are you doing here?" Katherine stammered, her eyes shifting between Raymond and Mr. Fixer, who was standing calmly next to his boss with a gun in one hand and a long, rusted rod in the other.

"We came to get you," Raymond said.

Katherine shook her head and closed her eyes. "How did you know—"

Before she could finish, Raymond cut her off. "The orb." He pointed to Lee. Lee dug into his pocket and pulled out the blue ball. "We've been listening," he continued.

"How?" Lee blurted. "I can barely make out anything even when I'm trying to hear it."

"We've done some fine-tuning here lately. When you reached out looking for Andrew, we were able to detect a message, like a foggy haze, but the intent was clear, and with some location tracking added on for good benefit, we knew where you'd be."

"I didn't think you could detect anything from the other side," Lee said.

Raymond smiled. "At first we couldn't, but with Clay whipping everyone into overtime, it actually worked out in our benefit. And we're not even supposed to have this." Mr. Fixer tossed another red orb from his front pocket to Raymond, who looked it over in his hands. "When we found out what Clay was doing, we realized we were in a position to help. At first, we played along, but as things got worse and people started dying, we had to work with a few members of your group. Daniel helped us get this rudimentary version, but I hear what they have in other areas is practically two-way, clear communication."

"Daniel's alive?" Lee blurted again. A large smile ran across Thomas's face, too.

"Yes, but . . ."

There's always a but, Katherine thought. She remembered Daniel from the research and development department, but she hadn't realized he had been working with Lee. She mentally added it to the list of things she had been in the dark about—and also things she didn't have time to focus on right now.

Raymond kept talking. "The only reason he still *is* alive is because Clay couldn't afford to kill him."

"What do you mean?" Lee asked, stepping forward, over Jeffrey, who still struggled on the ground, muttering something against his gag.

"Clay needs him," Raymond said. "After Ellen left, he was the smartest one in the department. He's basically been forced to cooperate or lose his life." Raymond kicked the ground. "What would you choose?"

"Where is he?" Thomas asked.

"In the lower levels, like everyone else. Clay moved everyone down there."

"How?" Katherine asked.

"There's barely enough room," Raymond said, looking toward Mr. Fixer. "It's pretty miserable down there, actually."

Katherine sighed. It was one thing to have a relatively small group of people to focus on saving, but now that the scope had expanded beyond their small group of people, they were basically being asked to do the impossible. Would it even be feasible to rescue everyone in the facility?

"And everyone else in the group?" Lee asked.

"Well, those that survived . . ."

Lee started tearing up.

". . . are down there, too, but Lee, you're not going to like it. If everyone thought things were bad before, they are immeasurably worse now."

Mr. Fixer nodded along. Katherine stared at him, wondering how he had been convinced to leave his relatively stable life and fight the same fight she was fighting, until it dawned on her that she had the same exact transformation not that long ago. Like her, his wheels were probably turning just as hard, evaluating every possible outcome. He might be quiet, but by his very nature, he was logical, meticulous, and plotting.

"It's not pretty," Raymond continued. "Even people like me and Andrew here are beaten for more productivity and control." His head dropped, and he stared at the ground. "We're just a handful of the lucky few who at least have *some* kind of good relationship with Clay. Not that it matters much."

"Well, what do we do?" Katherine asked. She stood in the middle of the hallway and stared at a ragtag group of individuals tasked with overthrowing Clay and saving the facility.

SIX

Grand Plan

"Do you think the group will be a problem?" Steven asked, standing in Richard's dining room.

Clay turned to him. "They better not be. Did you see that shot I got on that one guy? What is it? Paul, I think." Clay laughed. Steven tensed his whole body. "Anyway," Clay continued. "We've both got work to do. We'll set up main shop here, but I'll be back and forth a bit. Got some rather unpleasantness I have to deal with in Chicago, mostly."

"So you'll be using the command center."

Clay hung his jacket across a dining room chair. He smoothed out the sleeves before looking back at Steven with squinted eyes. "Of course." He stepped forward. "Look, I'm bringing you along for the journey, Steve. If you can't handle that, you have to let me know now. Do you understand?"

Steven gulped. It wasn't the journey he was worried about; it was his secret plan. Working with V to try and overthrow the facilities had him sweating more than normal. If Clay found out . . . He couldn't finish the thought.

"My wife will be asking questions, I'm sure," Steven lied.

"I'll be honest, I don't really care," Clay said.

"Yes, but—"

"What's the problem? Are you fully in . . . or not?"

It wasn't really a question. He had to be. He nodded. "Yes, sir."

"Then shut up. Look, I need my second-in-commands to come through. Until we have working comms between us, I've told them to keep an eye on things. The time to accelerate is here."

"Accelerate, sir?" Steven asked.

Clay cracked his neck. "Do you even know the full potential we're sitting on?" Spittle flew from the corner of his mouth and landed on Steven's shoulder. "Richard was holding us back. You know that more than anybody. He didn't even *try* to expand to any of the 'sketchy markets,' as he called them." Steven swore that if he didn't look away, Clay's eyes would bore a hole directly through his scalp. "Stupid," he exclaimed. "Like, do you even know what we're sitting on here? We could easily, without much effort, rule the country, if not the entire world!" Clay extended his arms upward.

Steven was unsure what to say or how to behave. Clay sounded like a madman, someone that Steven hadn't interacted with before. He had been around eccentric executives earlier in his career, but nothing quite like this. He felt he could always reason with Richard. With Clay, reasoning seemed to be a waste of breath.

"Productivity has skyrocketed since we took over. Even if we simply double, just *double*, what we are able to produce, it's a huge win. Can you imagine the leverage we'll have across the *world*?" Clay's eyes widened. "Not to mention the money!"

"You can't reasonably expect this to sustain itself."

"Why not?" Clay's stare pierced Steven's soul.

"People will die! We can't simply just bring more people on board. You, of all people, surely know how hard—"

"I fully acknowledge that some might die, and Steve, that's a risk we have to take for the full rewards."

What the facilities provided was above what anyone else was capable of. The technology was unmatched. There wasn't a need to ramp up production because they had what they needed, and it was dangerous. With Clay heading in this direction, and wanting even more, it made him more sadistic than Steven thought possible. They had run-ins and disagreements before, but being up close and personal with him in this moment made Steven realize that something had sprung loose in Clay's mind. Ever since murdering Richard and taking control, he wasn't the same person as before; he had somehow become even *more* maniacal. The sweat continued pouring down Steven's forehead; he had pinned all his hopes on a man he had never even met, the man on the external security group who was breaking Ayla and the rest free and hopefully coming back to rescue them all. In fact, he and V had only exchanged a handful of messages, the latest being from Steven's home office to set the plan in motion. In order to finally put an end to this madness, Steven had no option but to put his full trust in the relative stranger.

"So that's what I'm going to tell my commanders," Clay added.

"Tell them what, exactly?"

"To push forward. Aren't you paying attention?" He tapped Steven on the forehead. "I push my guys so they can push their facilities. It's a full takeover now."

"Didn't that not end well last time in—"

"I don't *care* about last time. This time is different! Pay attention. This *is* the endgame. This is where Richard didn't want to go; he didn't want to run them ruthlessly. But I'm telling you, it's the only place left. What good is all of this if we can't take total advantage of the situation? What was Richard going to do with it all anyway, huh?"

Steven shrugged. He had extended conversations with Richard but never knew the man's true intentions. He had been relatively even-keeled and calm the entire time they knew each other. Clay, on the other hand, was the opposite of that. He swore Clay's pupils dilated and went back to normal in a matter of seconds. Something was clearly wrong with the man standing in front of him.

SEVEN

Moving On

"I'll be honest," Ayla said, "I just don't think that's our best option."

"And I don't think we *have* any other options," the General said. "Unless, of course, we want to stay here and leave our fate in someone else's hands. If we don't act and move toward that door, those troops *will* come in here, *will* find and overpower us, and they absolutely *will* blow us away when they find out what we did to the Colonel."

"I'm surprised they haven't already," Derek said, standing over the unconscious guard on the ground.

"They're probably fighting off the rest of *your* troops." Ayla pointed her finger at the General.

"Good," he said. "Maybe there will be fewer of them when we storm out of here."

Ever since reconnecting with Derek, Ayla had felt a sense of security no matter the situation, but she was less than thrilled about being stranded in the middle of nowhere, waiting to die. The odds of getting out of here seemed to be dwindling with every passing minute, and it was just dumb luck that nobody had come to investigate the Colonel's absence yet. Their plan was fairly straightforward: run to the ornate door Thomas had once led her in from, somehow find out where that tunnel went, and lose the troops somewhere else in the facility. There were a lot of unknowns, assumptions, questions, and blind luck, but if everything broke their way, they would have a chance to regroup, reassess, and hopefully figure out how to get back to Chicago. Of course, still looming in Chicago was Ms. Ware, and who the hell knew what she was up to, but as far as Ayla was concerned, they were taking it one step at a time. There would be plenty of opportunity to keep piling stress on later.

Derek stepped toward the tent flap. "Ready?"

"Wait." Ayla turned to the General. "Can you go first?"

"Fine," he said, storming to the front of the tent.

An inquisitive look crawled across Derek's face.

Ayla shrugged. She was going to take every step she possibly could to make sure she and Derek stayed together and safe.

If she lost him again, she didn't know if she'd be able to manage.

If she lost him again, all the pain and suffering of what they had been through would be for nothing. She didn't want that thought to creep any further into her mind.

As the General swept the tent flap aside, loud popping and screaming came from outside. The General jumped back, let go of the tent flap, and snapped his gun to focus on the entrance. Derek stepped in front of Ayla. The General tiptoed forward, slid the barrel of his gun between the flaps, and peered out. Not more than ten seconds later, he pulled back and turned to Ayla and Derek.

"There seems to be some kind of . . . resistance . . . coming for us," he stammered.

"Resistance?" Derek asked.

Just when Ayla thought they were cornered and running out of time, there was yet *another* group coming to save the day that somehow had immaculate timing. She had found herself in all sorts of challenging, difficult, and seemingly impossible situations as of late but seemed to have luck on her side more often than not.

"I don't recognize three of them," the General said. "But it looks like they are with Katherine and Lee."

Ayla stomped forward.

"Ayla—" Derek reached for Ayla, just out of his grasp.

She held her fingers up to her lips to shoosh her boyfriend and peered out of the tent. Off in the distance, just past the pond, Katherine and Lee were sprinting straight for the tent. Next to them, she saw a larger man in overalls, lumbering his way alongside the group, with a weapon in each hand, protecting and shooting at whoever approached them. Next to the large man was a well-dressed, portly man, doing his best to keep up with the others. He would fall behind every now and again, but the large man made sure to pick him up and encourage him along. The last person was holding Lee's hand, stumbling next to him in the grass. Ayla squinted.

It couldn't be.

She had written him off as either dead or long forgotten. He was gangly and looked weak. His beard was longer than she remembered. Trotting alongside Lee was Thomas, the man who had led her to this miraculous hideout in the first place. The man who had nearly saved her life, only to be shot by Clay in the central square when she tried to save her boyfriend. She had blamed herself, so seeing him running through the field provided an unexpected jolt of energy and hope. She spun around as the tent flaps loosely shut against each other.

"It's Katherine, Lee, and one of the others is Thomas."

"Thomas?" Derek said. "Wasn't he the one who got shot?"

Ayla nodded. "It looks like he's here, though."

"Who are they with?" Derek asked.

"I don't know."

"What do you mean you don't know?" The General stepped forward.

"I've never seen those other two men before, but they're with Katherine and Lee, so they must be on our side, right?" She knew she was right, but the words came out formed like a question.

"A bold assumption with everything we've seen lately," the General said.

"I'll take whatever help we can get," Derek added.

"That's the other thing," Ayla said. "Your troops"—she looked at the General—"seem to be using the opportunity to fight back."

The General stuck his head out again.

"See them, by the treehouse?" she said without seeing the General's face. "And over by the pond?" She pictured it again, watching them slowly overcome their captors, some of them handcuffed and others falling to the ground, having their weapons torn away.

"You're right," the General said, returning to the tent. "It's not pretty, but you're right."

"So what are we waiting for?" Derek eagerly stepped to the front of the tent.

"Wait." Ayla reached out for him but just missed his arm. "They're coming for us," she added. "They were heading right for the tent. Let's hold tight and see what they want."

* * *

Thomas burst into the tent first. Derek and the General instinctively aimed their weapons at the man, who threw his hands straight up in the air.

"Wait," Ayla shouted. Then Lee and Katherine fumbled through the entrance, and Derek lowered his gun.

"Ayla, Derek!" Katherine cried out. She ran over and hugged Ayla. Lee followed close behind, a smile drawn on his face, throwing his arms around Ayla before moving on to Derek.

Thomas stood crooked by the front of the tent. "Thomas," she said. She threw her arms out to embrace the sick-looking man and grasped him like an egg. "I'm so happy to see you."

"You too, Ayla." Thomas coughed. "Thank you for coming back." A smile ran across his face, and Ayla could just make it out underneath his scraggly beard.

"I hate to spoil the mood." The General raised his voice, weapon still drawn and pointed at the tent opening. "But there are troops outside this tent that will be shortly behind our visitors here. I'm sure of it."

"He's right." The man in the disheveled suit stepped forward. "We don't have a lot of time."

Katherine held her hands up and signaled to everyone. "Everyone needs to lower their weapons."

"Who are these men?" the General asked.

"They're allies," Katherine said. "This is Raymond. He's the head of infrastructure and operations here for the facility."

"Used to be . . ." Raymond added.

"Right." Katherine took one step toward the man who towered above everyone else. "And this is Mr. Fixer." She paused before correcting herself. "I mean Andrew."

"Hello," he said.

Ayla jumped at his deep, booming voice.

Katherine finished his introduction. "He knows the ins and outs of most of the tech and can help us get out of here. And he," she continued, waving toward the General, "is the General. He helped us get here with some of his troops from another facility."

Raymond's eyes widened. "Another facility?"

"We don't have much time here," Ayla said.

"But wait," Raymond pleaded. "What do you mean by 'another facility'?"

It was probably a shock to Raymond, hearing about a world outside of the one he knew. Ayla likened it to when she first found out about *this* place. She wished there was enough time to set him aside and explain everything in detail, but that wasn't a luxury they currently had. She noticed Andrew's eyes widen, too, and she imagined he was in a similar situation.

"There are other facilities that do different things." Her eyes darted between Raymond and Andrew. "The General is from there, but we're kind of in a hurry. We'll explain more later." It was the best explanation she could think of on short notice.

"She's right." The General stepped forward and exchanged a brief glance with Derek. "We're stranded in the middle of a warzone without so much as a couple of guns."

"Understood," Raymond said as he nodded and tugged at his misbuttoned suit jacket. "I think your troops were able to surge when we showed up. I'm hoping we had something to do with it."

Standing near the tent flap, Ayla took the opportunity to peek out again. To her surprise, there were no troops running toward them and no ongoing battles like she had seen before. In fact, there were only a few people in total; the rest of the world seemed to be tucked away in the other sparse, makeshift tents. Ayla wasn't sure yet if that was a good or bad sign. She turned her attention back to the others, who were still discussing logistics and concerns over their current predicament. She caught Derek's eye, and they exchanged nods.

"Hey, guys." She raised her voice over the rest of the noise, indifferent to any ongoing conversations. With everyone's full attention, she continued. "I don't know what's going on out there, but whatever *was* happening seems to have died down, if not stopped entirely."

"What?" The General's voice had a weird inflection as he strode across the ground and stuck his head out of the tent flap. "She's right," he said mere seconds later.

Ayla threw her hands up in the air. *Of course I'm right.*

"What does that mean?" Derek asked.

"I'm not . . . I'm not sure," the General stuttered.

"It means we have to go," Lee said. "We have to get out of here."

"We have to have some kind of plan, Lee," Katherine said.

"I think we need to get back to Chicago and regroup. We clearly weren't prepared for whatever the hell it is we walked into here."

"Clay's trap . . ." Thomas, who had been mostly quiet in the corner up until now, managed to eke out a few words.

"I'm sorry?" the General said.

"Clay planned this whole thing."

"He knew we were coming back?" the General asked.

Thomas just nodded.

"People are suffering," Raymond said, practically out of the blue. "In the lower levels. We can't just leave them."

"We can come back," Lee added.

"No," Thomas added weakly. "We can't risk it. They could be dead by the time we get back." He coughed into his hand.

"He's right." Derek's armor jangled as he stepped toward the rest of the group. He had been quiet lately, too, which was outside his normal mode of operation. Ayla thought it was because he was formulating a plan, but it seemed as though he was being extra analytical. "We worked damn hard to get down here and can't just run back at the first sign of trouble."

"This is a bit more than I'd call trouble," the General added.

Derek continued without addressing the General. "And it sounds like there could be another surprise waiting for us back in Chicago."

"Chicago?" Raymond asked.

"Another facility," Ayla added as Raymond bit his lip, holding back more questions.

"We need to rescue those below and get out of here so that Clay doesn't do this to the rest of the facilities. He's too dangerous of a person to roam free." Derek looked over at Ayla. "Believe me . . ."

"What are you suggesting?" The General asked.

"We split up. We take whatever troops are left out there"—Derek gestured toward the tent flap—"and divide and conquer. Half take the lower levels, half go back to Chicago to try and warn others."

"What if Chicago's a trap, too?" Lee asked.

"I'm not worried about Chicago," the General added. "My men, my responsibility."

Derek kept talking. "Plus, Ellen should be there to help, right?"

Ayla and Katherine both nodded in sync, signifying an unexpected vote of confidence in Ellen.

"So how do we want to do this?" Ayla was asking the obvious question but knew it had to be stated. She disliked the idea of splitting the group up again after it had worked so hard to come together.

* * *

"Raymond and Andrew, you know the lower levels the best," Derek said.

Raymond nodded.

"You lead that group with myself and some troops. General, you take Ayla, Thomas, Katherine, and Lee back to Chicago."

"Absolutely not," Ayla chimed in. She was half a second away from stomping her foot on the ground. "There's no way I'm leaving you by choice."

Derek's head collapsed into his hand, and he rubbed his forehead. "Ayla, we don't have time for this."

"We absolutely have time for this," Ayla insisted, getting to within a few inches of Derek's face. "I know full well what happens when we split up, and there's no way I'm going for it again."

"Ayla, we have strength in numbers this time and we know where each other is going to be. It's entirely different; you're not sneaking off in the middle of the night."

Ayla's gut wrenched and twisted.

Did he just say that?

When she left on that autumn night, out to innocently explore an abandoned building and take some photographs, she didn't know she'd stumble onto a mystery that called to her. Later, when she left to explore that weird hatch with the odd symbols, she hadn't meant to get into this mess. She was only looking for something new, something fun—an adventure. She had finally gotten over that sick feeling of getting into this entire situation to begin with, and now he was bringing it back up all over again. Maybe he didn't mean to, but he should be more aware of the situation than to twist that knife in further.

She sighed. "Derek, this is not negotiable."

The General cleared his throat. "As much as I enjoy a good love story, this is not something we can be distracted with right now. I will go to the lower levels. I can lead my troops down there; it's like a normal mission for us."

"And I'd like to stay here." Lee looked around. "Kind of finish what I started, you know?"

"What is there to finish?" Thomas said. "There's literally nothing left, Lee. There's nothing to fight for. There are those in the lower levels, but at this point, let's worry more about ourselves."

"Thomas is right," Derek added. "It's more important to get ourselves back to Chicago at the moment and save ourselves."

"And the other facilities?" Ayla said. "Is everyone forgetting that we're not the center of the world here?" She generically pointed outside of the tent. "There are other facilities out there, with other unwilling people. Maybe Clay has them trapped, too. Maybe he's got an army of slaves. Maybe he's thinking world domination or something. Who knows? The problem now *is* that nobody knows. Nobody knows about the problems here, nobody knows about the other facilities, nobody seems to know anything. Where I come from, up above, nobody knows about the issues here. Does anyone else find that to be a problem?"

The group fell silent. Ever since Ayla first found out about the other facilities, in Clay's control room, she couldn't shake them from her brain.

Who were they?

What were they doing?

Why were they there?

The fact that nobody else seemed concerned about them was disheartening. She didn't come all this way to simply stop caring about people. They had as good a plan as any for the people here in the lower levels, but it seemed like nobody had considered everyone else.

Katherine started circling the group. "They have to be similar to us. Except, I would imagine, that they probably focus on other things. Research things, right?"

"She's right," the General said. "As I understand it, because Chicago was in charge of defense, we had a bit more insight into the others, and I know for a fact they were all researching different technologies. But that's not particularly relevant right now, is it?"

"Fascinating," Raymond muttered.

"We just have to figure out how to free them," Ayla said.

"Hold on," the General said. "Why are we freeing them?"

Ayla's eyes widened. She couldn't believe what she was hearing. "Because we have an obligation now."

"We have no indication they are in trouble. The only reason we're here"—he pointed to the ground—"is because you showed up and told us the horrors going on here. There are no such stories for the others."

"That doesn't mean we shouldn't—"

"Hey . . ." Mr. Fixer's deep voice cut off Ayla. "We need to make a move." He was peering outside the tent. "There seems to be a problem out there."

"Let's reconvene once we're back in Chicago."

Ayla conceded. There simply wasn't enough time to continue arguing in the tent. She relaxed her shoulders. This wasn't a fight she could win in the middle of an escalating situation, and she wasn't going to convince anyone in this environment.

Derek checked his gun. "Okay, I will lead the group back to Chicago." He looked over at the General. "Are you good with taking on the lower levels with our new friends here?" He nodded to Raymond and Mr. Fixer. The General simply nodded. Derek leaned in and kissed Ayla. A warm comfort washed over her, and all the cares of the others slipped away momentarily, until Derek pulled his lips away.

EIGHT

Treehouse Troubles

The vein in Derek's neck pulsed against his skin. He had gotten better at ignoring it, but it was something he always sensed. He wouldn't call it anger, specifically. More disappointment. Disappointment in Ayla for not trusting him to return her to safety. In Chicago, he was able to quickly earn the trust of the General, going so far as to lead a squad to the treehouse in Kansas City. He saw no reason his girlfriend would think he'd be unable to lead the charge into the lower levels and return Ayla to safety.

He guessed he couldn't entirely blame her, even if the vein in his neck thought otherwise. Given everything that had transpired lately, it wasn't entirely her fault. While she technically was the one who snuck out at night to find the abandoned warehouse, only to follow some weird tunnel and end up in this crazy underground world, he also empathized with her desire to escape the mundane.

The tiny apartment.

The shitty job.

The so-so boyfriend.

He was hard on himself, but after having a bit of time to reflect on everything, he realized he probably wasn't providing the best he could for her. She had a hard life and a hard past. Abandonment issues with her father crept into conversations and situations he didn't expect. She needed someone to trust. Derek liked to think he was up to the task, but lately, he had been second-guessing himself. So even though his vein was disappointed in Ayla, the more he thought about it, the more he thought that maybe he was just disappointed in himself.

Many thoughts swirled through Derek's head as he led the group through the grassy hills that had long since been cleared out by the General and the remaining Chicago troops. The troops had swept the area and left to take the battle to the lower levels. They had overpowered the Colonel's, and Clay's, men. Derek and the rest of the group watched from the tent, hope growing with each battle won, and optimism found its way back to Derek's heart. The hope didn't last long, though, as an intrusive thought pried its way into Derek's brain—the thought of letting Ayla down once again. He took a deep breath. Although this mission was relatively easy, sometimes even the most straightforward work encountered hiccups.

The group finally reached the intricately carved staircase of the treehouse. He stepped aside and let the rest of the group past him, covering them as they ran up the steps. Lee was the last one through, patting Derek's shoulder as he passed, and they exchanged a look of satisfaction. For a brief moment, Derek felt like he had found another purpose beyond his mundane life above: saving people and leading them to freedom. Something to escape the everyday monotony of life. He finally felt happy. Then he heard Katherine scream from upstairs.

He bounded up the steps two at a time until he reached the top. He threw his helmet off and it made a thud against the hard walnut floor. Lee was standing next to their escape portal, but instead of glowing red, it was a black, inky nothingness. Flashbacks of his experience in the interrogation room with Clay leaped to his mind. Clay had slammed his hand against the door leading to the pit, the dark black, lifeless portal. He instinctively shook his hand out, which still didn't feel quite normal. The hair stood up on his neck, and goosebumps exploded down his arms.

He shoved Lee and Thomas out of the way until he made his way next to Katherine and Ayla, standing face to face with the black portal. "What the hell is this?"

"I don't know," Katherine said.

"It looks just like the pit." He exchanged looks with Ayla. "Clay tortured me with this thing, but what the hell is it doing here?"

"It's not *the* pit," Lee said from behind.

"Where is our portal back to Chicago?"

"This *could* go back to Chicago, right? What if it just . . . changed . . ." Thomas said, his inflection betraying his doubt.

"I'm not fucking going in there," Derek said, pointing at the portal.

"Yeah," Ayla added. "We just pushed the Colonel through the one in the tent." She gulped. "It didn't look . . . great."

Lee addressed the rest of the group. "Then what do we do?"

Derek kicked the floor and dropped his head. "This is unbelievable!"

"Do you think it's Ellen?" Katherine asked.

Lee shrugged, and his brow furrowed. "I wouldn't put it past her."

"No way," Ayla said. "She wouldn't do that to us."

"I know I just said we could trust her, but now that I think about it, this is definitely something she would do. At least the old Ellen." Katherine side-eyed Ayla.

"What if it was Ms. Ware?" Ayla asked. "What if she was working with Clay this whole time?"

Lee gasped. "Raymond and Mr. Fixer. The lower levels. Did we just send them into another trap?"

"But they've been down there; they know what they're walking into," Ayla added.

"The General doesn't," Lee said.

Katherine stepped forward. "But nobody's after the General. And Raymond and Mr. Fixer have been working with us, remember?"

Derek wasn't sure who to trust anymore, but he didn't like the situation. "Look," he said. "There's no point in us trying to help them. Worst case, it's a trap and we're ensnared in it. Best case, they save everyone and escape anyway. There's no use in us adding to it. We need to focus on finding a way back to Chicago like we all agreed on."

"I don't know if that's such a good idea anymore," Ayla said. "What if Ms. Ware's waiting for us there?"

"What other options do we have?"

"Well . . ." Katherine said weakly. "We could find our way back to Clay's command center. Remember, the place with all those other doors?"

"But what about Raymond and Mr. Fixer and the General and everyone in the lower levels?" Lee stomped his foot. "This is a disaster all over ag—"

"No," Derek cut in. "This isn't a disaster. This *can't* be a disaster." This was something he was fully in control of. He just had to think for a second.

"Derek—"

"Ayla." Derek cut off his girlfriend. Ayla took a step back. Derek rubbed his temples. The vein in his neck started saying hello.

"The command center is the only option," Katherine said again.

"I agree," Lee said.

"And we've been there before," Ayla reminded the group. "Remember, when we were down there but had to leave because of whatever was coming after us?" She reached her arm toward Derek. "It's not there. It's a reasonable escape plan."

Derek sighed. He was starting to come to that conclusion, too, but didn't want to admit it. Diverging from the plan could have impacts beyond what they had considered. He knew how the General's mind worked, and a divergence in the plan could be detrimental, but the tradeoffs for all other options didn't make sense. The mission had suddenly turned more difficult, and he laughed internally about how he once thought this was going to be easy. He stopped pacing and snapped his attention back to the group. Ayla, Lee, Thomas, and Katherine were all staring at him as if he had gone crazy, their eyes wide, their faces strained with anticipation.

"We have to move quickly," he said.

NINE

Ruins

All this time, Ayla had thought what she needed was an adventure. The old hatch in the warehouse signified that for her, and she had taken it. It led to an exciting place full of mysteries. But all that excitement couldn't fill a void inside of her. A void her father had left a long time ago. A void of abandonment, and when she was with Derek, she didn't feel that; she felt safe. The sense of safety surrounded her as she followed closely behind Derek, running through the abandoned library. They had taken one of the less formidable portals out of the treehouse and found themselves in a room similar to where Thomas had taken Ayla when he helped her escape the hospital: small, cramped, full of boxes for some reason, but out of the way enough to be a secret passage. There was a hidden ladder in the floor that dropped down to the top level of the library. Once they had all climbed down, Lee, the tallest of the group, propped the retracted ladder into place and carefully put the ceiling panel back.

Derek grabbed Lee and used his existing knowledge of the library to guide everyone.

The top floor was what Ayla was most expecting: a normal library with endless shelves and books. When they reached the staircase, it became apparent this was not a normal library. The stairs were burned and charred, chipped and scratched. The damage only became worse as they went down. The next floor down looked like a war-torn storage room. Ripped-apart books were scattered across the floor, and most of the shelves were tipped over. Smoldering remains of piles of books lit their way, and burn marks scorched the walls. Rugs that once lined the hardwood floors were strewn about and pulled apart. There were holes in the ceiling where lights once hung. The group wound their way down the staircase, the damage increasing at each level, until they finally reached the bottom. They maneuvered around more scattered trash and a shattered chandelier on their way toward the door against the far wall. What Ayla imagined had once been a place of great creativity was now eroded, and she couldn't help but feel it was her fault.

She was the one who came in and blew up their way of life.

She was the one who forced Clay's hand.

She was the one responsible for it all. She felt a hand drop on her shoulder. It was Katherine.

"It's okay," Katherine said, smiling.

Has she been reading my mind?

"I know." It was all Ayla could muster up to say.

"This would have happened with or without you." She paused to take a breath and check her footing. "It was only a matter of time." She patted Ayla's shoulder twice.

"Thanks," Ayla said between breaths. While it was probably true, it didn't make her feel much better in the moment, as they found their way to the door, a few jewels hanging off the top, once a piece of art that now stood as a reminder of the ruinous nature of humanity. Ayla briefly paused and sighed before picking up her pace and following the group again.

An ominous silence fell over them as they made their way to the middle of the central square. Ayla shuddered, remembering what had happened here in the past. Clay's maniacal eyes flashed in front of her. The look on his face as he pointed his gun at Derek and counted down would forever be seared into her memory. Never in a million years did she think she'd be back here, but as she looked around now, it was hard to deny the tragedies that had taken place. The displaced people. The damage to a breathtaking facility. Everything had fallen.

As the group slowed, everyone eyed a pile of rubble in the middle of the space. Where once stood the Beacon, the tower that protruded from the ground and Ayla remembered from her encounter with Clay, was now just a crater. It was a haunting reminder of the atrocities that Clay had committed. It sent shivers down Ayla's back, only made worse by the coolness of the air, much cooler than before. Ayla remembered the sunlight portal hanging high above, which was now nowhere to be seen. The lack of light sent the entire space into an ominous darkness, extending dark shadows up and down the walls. The trash that littered the place last time she was here was piled even higher now, and the group had to weave through the area to get to the elevator.

Lee reached for the call button, but Derek stopped him.

"What?" Lee asked.

"Are we sure this is safe?" Derek turned to Lee, Katherine, and Thomas, all bunched together by the elevator button.

"Why wouldn't it be?" Lee asked.

"The General and troops are already there," Katherine added. "Based on what they did at the treehouse, they've probably taken over the whole area by now."

"I just . . ." Derek bit his lip. "I don't know."

Katherine smashed the elevator button. The old, creaky elevator door lurched to life, slowly opening and sending groans and moans through the rest of the central square, ricocheting off the heaps of garbage.

"This feels like a bad idea now," Ayla said. Even though she had brought it up, heading back to the lower levels to reach the command center door seemed like a poorly thought-out plan. She didn't know much about the lower levels other than the last time she was down there. Endless halls of doors, being chased by someone, ducking into Shirley's room.

Shirley . . .

Ayla held back tears. Derek reacted and threw his arm around her waist.

"We don't have a choice, right?" Lee asked.

"Right," Katherine added. "It's how we get back to the command center."

As the doors continued to open, Derek stepped in front of Ayla. Ayla swore the doors were faster last time. She peeked her head around Derek's shoulder and into the empty elevator. She let out a deep breath, as did Derek.

"Katherine's right. We have to head that way." Without

hesitation, Derek stepped into the elevator and pulled Ayla with him.

They only found an empty space where the controls once were. Wires sparked and jutted outward. All of the internal controls had been destroyed.

Derek slammed his fist against the metallic side and sent a shock wave through the enclosed space.

TEN

Inner Turmoil

Ellen's room was simple: a small bed and end table in one corner and a three-shelf drawer in the other. There were no windows. Instead, just a single overhead bulb illuminated the cinder blocks. It was a far cry from the luxurious office she once had as a powerful position holder in the Kansas City facility, a leader of a renowned group, a first-class citizen living above everyone else, with access to everything, including people. She sat on the bed and ran her hand across the rough, mud-colored comforter and sighed. It was less than ideal.

Her conversation with Ms. Ware didn't inspire confidence, and when she reflected on everything she had accomplished, not just here but back in Kansas City, she realized it was all part of a bigger plan she couldn't see. She hated being in a position that wasn't in control, and no matter what she tried to do lately, she seemed to always find herself captured in someone else's web. She thought she'd be escaping Clay and getting the upper hand for once but now realized he *always* had the upper hand and she was yet again his pawn. She balled her hand into a fist and punched the puke-colored bed. She let out a scream; it bounced around the boring walls and died in an empty silence.

She took a deep breath.

Her hand started to shake and she hit the bed again. She felt a tugging in the corners of her eyes but wiped any traces of tears away as soon as they formed. For no reason in particular, she found her mind wandering off to her old assistant, Sam, and the way she left him for dead in the command center. She had escaped Kansas City with Katherine and Lee and the others, and for some reason, she thought leaving him behind to protect them as they escaped again was the best course of action. Without warning, tears flooded down her face and she could no longer control them, another unfamiliar and uncomfortable feeling. She shoved her head into the pillow and let her tears drench the pillowcase. She squished herself into the pillow further to muffle and dampen her cries as much as she could. She felt like she was smothering herself, which, for a brief moment, she thought wouldn't be the worst way out of this situation. She cried until it felt like she was dehydrated and couldn't possibly cry anymore. She pulled her head away from the pillow and the once-brown color had turned nearly black, covered in tears. She sniffed and dabbed at her eyes with the back of her hands.

Ellen sat upright and straightened her back. She inhaled deeply, sucking in the stale air she had become all too familiar with. Without portals, this facility was still reliant on the old circulatory systems, sun lamps, and other older technology she had long ago forgotten. She couldn't live this way anymore. She had to get back to where she belonged. She had to be running the game, not sitting on the sidelines, crying into her pillow. She licked her lips. The coolness of her tears was refreshing, and that's when she decided to reach for a glass of dirt-tasting water on the bedside table. She downed the entire glass without a second thought and cleared her throat.

She turned up the burners in her analytical mind and logically laid out the options.

Staying here and helping Ms. Ware as much as she could seemed viable, but she strongly disliked the idea of helping Ms. Ware, and it wasn't clear to her if Ms. Ware was in charge or if Clay would be in charge. The task was also impossible. Two-way portals were a huge achievement in itself, and now she was expected to do the same with the orbs. Maybe some of what she had accomplished could work with the orbs, but with merely two days to get them working, it felt like a trap. Besides, if Clay was the one actually in charge, Ellen feared she wouldn't last long, and she wasn't too fond of being held captive by anyone right now.

Running off on her own was another option. However, this one had the most unknowns. Ever since she discovered Ms. Ware and Clay working together, she had prepared with her secret portal, but she couldn't imagine the idea of using that portal to flee somewhere she didn't know and expect to thrive. She'd be a nobody in a mystery land. She'd be starting from scratch, in strange territory. She shook the thought from her mind. It was an option she had to consider, but it was not her favorite by a long shot.

A mere fleeting option was continuing to suffocate in her pillow. A perhaps quicker and more merciful way to go than to run into Clay again. The thought passed briefly, and Ellen didn't seriously consider it.

The last option, and the option that started to look more favorable as time went on, was meeting up with Ayla and Derek again and helping them. It would achieve a couple of goals, not the least of which was putting Clay in his rightful spot. It could also serve to vault Ellen back to a prestigious position. She daydreamed about one day being talked about as "the person who overthrew Clay." She didn't let her mind wander too far down that path, but she liked the option more than most. While she doubted Katherine or Lee would welcome her with open arms, it seemed as though they'd at least have a common goal to rally around, similar to when they escaped Kansas City together. It would take her a couple of days to finalize details for her personal portal, so she'd have to figure out how to balance that while feigning some sort of progress on Ms. Ware's request. With the lab basically to herself, and without prying eyes, she figured it wouldn't be too difficult.

Ellen stood and smoothed out her blanket and fluffed her pillow. She waltzed to the dingy mirror and cleaned up her face. "This could work," she said out loud. "This *will* work. Soon enough, you'll be back on top." After waiting for the redness in her face to subside and her heart rate to slow, she walked out of her room and headed for the lab.

ELEVEN

Katherine in Charge

Katherine wished she had paid more attention to her colleagues over the years. Getting to know Raymond would have been beneficial, and she kicked herself for avoiding the lower levels as much as possible. When Ayla first arrived and she brought her stuff to Mr. Fixer, her goal was to get in and out as fast as possible. If only she had spent more time with him, maybe she would have realized he was working with Lee. Even her conversations with Ellen were sparse, although she was still convinced the woman hated her for no apparent reason. But now she was stuck looking for a way to get out, and any other information would have helped.

She turned to Lee and Thomas and interrupted their whispering spat. "Do you guys remember anything else? Any other ways out?"

"Unfortunately no," Lee said.

"What about your original plan to escape with the group at the treehouse?"

"We'd need Daniel"—Lee looked at the ceiling above where the Beacon once was—"and the Mirror for that to work . . ."

The once-reflective and beautiful portal known as the Mirror, which hung above the Beacon, had been powered down, and all that hung in the sky was a shattered, dull, saucer-like chandelier ominously staring down below at the abandoned central square.

"Ayla or Derek." Katherine turned her attention their way. "Did you see anything else while you were here, maybe in the lower levels? Any . . . place or anything that would help us get out of here?"

"Like I said earlier," Derek chimed in, "the only place I saw was the interrogation room with the pit, but other than that, no."

Katherine raised her eyebrows. "Ayla?"

"I saw a machinery level, a home level . . . but nothing that would really help."

"We might be out of options." Katherine's voice quavered. The wasteland they were surrounded by offered little hope. Her internal compass had always been good, like when she tried to do what was right by Ayla when she first showed up, but now, it seemed that she had made a wrong choice somewhere. Conversations of following protocol with Jeffrey ran through her mind, and now she wondered if she could have avoided all of this by listening to her colleague.

Her train of thought came to a screeching halt.

"Jeffrey!" she practically yelled.

Lee slapped his forehead loud enough to send an echo throughout the space. "Of course!" he exclaimed. "Why didn't I think of that?"

Thomas started laughing.

"Can someone tell me what's going on?" Derek asked, his arm wrapped around Ayla's waist.

Katherine's eyes lit up. A plan was starting to formulate in her brain. "We ran into Jeffrey in the hospital wing when we rescued Thomas." She had the full attention of the group now, gathered near the elevator to listen. "Raymond and Mr. Fixer helped overpower him and the guards so we could get out of there."

"What's your point?" Derek asked shortly.

"My point is," Katherine continued, "that we left them there, chained to the hospital beds, locked in the rooms. We can use Jeffrey to help us get out of here."

"How can we be sure he knows a way out?" Ayla asked.

"When we left—and, more importantly, when *Ellen* left—Jeffrey became Clay's right-hand man. He's been helping Clay with"—Katherine paused and looked around at the trash heaps—"whatever happened to this place. Thomas, you even saw it for yourself, right?"

Thomas simply nodded.

"Make sense," Lee added. He threw his arm around Thomas's shoulder and gave it a light squeeze. "When he interfered down here with our whole debacle . . ." He shot a look to Katherine. Lee didn't have to clarify; she still clearly remembered being at the top of the Beacon, trying to give a warning to Lee and Ayla that Clay was coming for them, only to find herself cornered and betrayed by Jeffrey, who slapped restraints on her wrists and turned her in. "Clay's 'trust-o-meter' probably went off the charts for Jeffrey. How many people have gone out of their way to help him before?"

"Exactly," Katherine said.

"I'll be honest," Derek said. "I don't remember a lot about those events, but what makes you so sure he knows a way out?"

"He must," Lee said. "Right?"

Katherine nodded. "Ellen met with Clay in the supply room, remember?" Katherine's memory wasn't great, but she did recall at least part of a conversation with Ellen about her meetings with Clay. "If she met with him there, Jeffrey probably meets him there, too. It was the room we used to escape the first time, the one that led us to the command center." Katherine looked around. "Jeffrey knows about it. Maybe he has another way there, right? He must."

The group didn't respond except for a couple of shoulder shrugs.

Katherine kept talking. "I just don't know. None of us know. But Jeffrey *might*. Besides, what other options do we have?"

* * *

Katherine found herself in the lead, ducking and weaving through the garbage in the central square. She passed a familiar-looking tent where she was pretty sure she had coffee before, but there was no time to stop and inspect. They were on their way to the hospital wing, where Jeffrey was locked to a bed. They needed him, and as much as it pained Katherine to admit that they needed him, it was for the better of the group, so she didn't take it so personally. She didn't think he would play a major role in her life much anymore, but things always had a funny way of working out like that.

The group approached the oversized doors with a large white cross. Typically, they'd be closed, but with all the issues and power-routing problems, they were now cracked open enough that they could fit through. They all slid through the opening, one by one, until they stood in the dilapidated lobby, once full of overstuffed cushions and semi-clean floors, now nothing but tossed furniture and rubble. Katherine was powering forward but was stopped by Derek's voice.

"I think it's best if I stay here," Derek said. "I can be on lookout."

It was a good idea, in case any more of Clay's men showed up, but she hated being separated as a group, especially now that they were so close to getting out of here.

"That might be for the best," Thomas said. "When I was here, there was a main patrol, but I'm not sure if they send backup or if anyone else would come through."

"Okay, fine," Katherine said.

Ayla was quick to jump in. "I'm staying, too."

Katherine sighed. "That's fine. Anyone else?" The group remained silent. "Then we'll meet you back here in ten minutes."

Derek nodded.

"Wait," Ayla said. "What if you're not back in ten minutes?"

The question hung in the air like the once-active Mirror in the central square, lingering and imposing, and nobody really knew how to address it.

"I guess—" Katherine started to say.

"What room are you in?" Derek interrupted. "If you're not here in ten minutes, we'll come find you."

"Down this hallway," Katherine said, pointing the way. "Take a right at the end. Then, when you come to the first hallway, take a left. We're a handful of doors down that way, off to the right. I don't remember the exact room."

"Got it," Derek said, looking over at Ayla and nodding.

Katherine headed down the hall surrounded by the glow of the backup emergency lights. She had only seen them on one other time and had never expected to see them again. But once again, she was back in territory she didn't want to be in. Lee and Thomas were close behind her, maneuvering between Katherine's footsteps. The garbage seemed to get worse with every step, something that Katherine must have blocked out when she and Lee first came through here. There was nothing redeeming about her old place of work anymore, and she wanted to get out of here as fast as possible. In the past, she'd dream about being holed up in her office, being able to evaluate patients all day. Reality and crazy schedules often got in the way of that, and now she couldn't imagine spending even one more minute in this run-down building. So while some things stayed the same and found their way back into her life, most other things changed, almost too quickly. If it was this different up here, she could only imagine the lower levels and how Raymond, Mr. Fixer, and the General were holding up.

Have we made a mistake?

Should we have regrouped and tried again?

Could we have done things differently?

Lee's voice broke her train of thought. "Katherine," he said.

She stopped, realizing she had walked right past the door they needed. "Sorry." She backtracked to where Thomas and Lee were waiting. "Lost in thought, I guess." She managed to eke out a meager smile. She reached for the backup locking mechanism on the doors, near the top of the doorframe, and a clicking sound meant the door was open. Katherine was the first to step inside.

"Long time no see," Jeffrey said, sitting in the hospital bed just where they had left him. "And you brought the whole gang," he added as Lee and Thomas filed in behind Katherine. "Where's Raymond and Mr. Fixer? Did they decide to dump you off?" He smiled.

"Jeffrey," Katherine said, walking over to one of the bedside tables. "We need to talk." She kept her eyes on him the whole time as she reached the table and grabbed a loose cigarette they had confiscated from him. She opened the drawer and grabbed the lighter, lit the cigarette, and held it out. "Before I give you this," she continued, "can you promise that you'll answer our questions?"

"That depends entirely, doesn't it?" he asked. "What do your questions pertain to?"

"Clay," Katherine lied. It wasn't entirely a lie, as it was semi-related to Clay, but she knew Jeffrey wouldn't flat-out help them escape.

"Clay?" Jeffrey laughed. "What *about* Clay?"

"Is that a yes?"

Jeffrey opened the palm of his hand from its clasped position on the bed. Katherine took that as a good sign. "What do you need to know?" he asked, taking the cigarette from Katherine's hand. His first drag was a long one, and Katherine let him enjoy it. He blew smoke toward the ceiling and turned his attention back to Katherine. "Thank you," he said.

"We need to see him," Katherine said. Lee provided an encouraging nod from across the room. "Immediately."

"Wow," Jeffrey said. "Never thought I'd hear you say that." He took another puff from his cigarette. "Going for the same, well-oiled strategy that worked for you last time?"

"Don't be a smartass. I know you see him regularly. How? How do *we* get ahold of him?"

Jeffrey laughed. "What, do you think he's just going to show up and have a nice conversation with you?"

Katherine snatched the cigarette from between his fingers, threw it onto the dirty floor, and crushed it with her shoe. Jeffrey's face twisted like she had taken away a toy from a child.

He raised his voice. "How dare you!"

"I'm not screwing around," Katherine responded. "He'll talk to you, won't he? How do you do it?" She watched his face twist even more, agonizing every second he didn't have that cigarette. His stained-yellow teeth were grinning through his tightened lips.

"Fine," he groaned. "There's a portal in Ellen's old office. It goes to the supply room."

Katherine breathed a sigh of relief.

"But it's not that simple," he said. "It's guarded. You can't just walk through it, you know?"

"No, I don't know," Katherine said. "Enlighten me."

"There's a screen, and a code, and a person on the other side has to approve. It's a whole ordeal. It's a protocol."

The way he said "protocol" rubbed Katherine the wrong way. She gritted her teeth and grabbed Jeffrey's wrist. "You're coming with us."

* * *

Jeffrey coughed and made a big scene as Derek held him by the handcuffs and dragged him through the hospital lobby.

"Slow down, please," he begged at one point.

Katherine didn't even feel like turning around to acknowledge him. She'd had enough of this and was ready to get the hell out of this nightmare. Raymond and Mr. Fixer hadn't beaten him up too badly, and although the guards he was with protested from the other sides of their locked hospital rooms, Jeffrey was quick to tell them it was okay. Probably because he knew he didn't really have an option. He was at their mercy now, and it was a nice change of pace from when Jeffrey held Katherine in handcuffs. She thought she was being smart by taking decisive action with her call out from the Beacon, to give Lee and Ayla a leg up, but in retrospect, she regretted the choice. If she hadn't alerted them, and Jeffrey hadn't turned against her, she'd still be in the inner circle.

Maybe she could have helped more from the inside.

Maybe everyone else would have escaped.

Maybe she would have turned on Jeffrey and gotten on Clay's side. Maybe that wouldn't have been a good thing.

Maybe they *were* doing the right thing.

Lots of maybes ran through her head.

She sighed.

If only she did *this*, or if only she had done *that*, or maybe now they needed to go *here* instead of *there* . . .

It had all become a bit too much.

She tried to focus back on the moment. "This way," she called back to the group falling behind her. They were headed for the *other* elevator in the central square, the one that went up. In the past, it had strict security, and by security, Katherine didn't mean Clay's team, but rather like a "keeper of the upper levels." Above the central square were offices and housing for the well-off, although that definition seemed to change depending on who and when you asked. There used to be an entire other housing floor above, but with Clay's "incident" all that time ago, those units had been wiped out and were used for nothing, sitting entirely empty. It was a long way up, and while the stairs were *technically* an option, too, Katherine couldn't remember the last time she saw someone use the decrepit-looking and now-likely-in-disrepair staircase. Long ago she had heard rumors that the Beacon was the base of an even older stairwell that used to spiral up and out to all of the floors, but she never was able to confirm that.

Katherine reached the elevator first and slid open the gate blocking off the entrance. She confirmed the controls were intact, so she and the group were already better off than they were with their first plan. She corralled everyone inside, slammed the gate shut, locked the door, and punched the button for the top floor. The elevator rumbled and clanked its rusty bones up the floors.

Jeffrey broke the silence. "Could I trouble anyone for a cigarette?"

Katherine glared at him. "Actually, yes, that would be trouble." The central square got smaller and smaller the further they rose. She wanted to know how the rest of the group was doing and feeling and reacting to having Jeffrey in their midst but thought it would be more imposing and intimidating to maintain her staunch pose. The last thing she needed was for Jeffrey to think he could just walk all over her; she wasn't going to let anything like that happen again.

The elevator finally cranked its way to their floor and stammered to a halt. Jeffrey, in his overdramatic acting, fell to his knees and acted like he hit his face. Even if he did, Katherine didn't care. She rushed to open the steel cage again and let the rest of the group out, trying not to make eye contact with Jeffrey as Derek pulled him to his feet. The group paused briefly on the catwalk overlooking the rest of the central square below until Katherine closed the elevator again and stepped out to join them on the narrow walkway. They had to all stand next to each other against the wrought-iron railing to let Katherine through.

"The office is just up this way, not too far now," she said.

They hiked halfway down one walkway until they reached a corner and kept going. About halfway down this walkway was Ellen's old office—or, rather, the office for whoever was the head of research and development, a position Katherine assumed was now taking applicants. There was an oversized portrait window that opened out to the walkway and down below, and alongside it stood a door that was once locked but had now fallen off its hinges. The office was nearly three times the size of a normal housing cubicle in the upper levels. Katherine thought back to her hand-me-down, semi-recycled, wobbly furniture in her dingy office and shuddered. Inside the once-luxurious office were papers strewn about, books askew on the shelves, and an overturned desk. "What happened here?" she asked no one in particular. None of the lights inside seemed to work, and the extravagant office was lit only by the dimness rising from the central square below.

Katherine signaled to Jeffrey. "Show us the way."

"What do I get out of it?" Jeffrey kicked a piece of trash away from his foot.

"I'm sorry?" Katherine inched forward.

Jeffrey looked around the room. "You all clearly need me, but what's in it for me?"

"What's in it for you?"

Shit. Katherine wasn't expecting him to negotiate. She had gotten so wrapped up in taking charge she hadn't realized she had next to no leverage. Katherine jumped back when she saw Jeffrey crumple over. It took her a minute to process that Derek had jabbed him in the side.

Ayla grabbed Derek's arm. "What are you doing?" she asked.

"You don't get to negotiate," Derek barked at Jeffrey.

"Actually," Jeffrey wheezed from one knee, "I think I do. I'm the only route you have to Clay, and it seems like you need me and my services a hell of a lot more than I need you."

Katherine exchanged looks with Derek. She cocked her head to the side, and Derek's shoulders briefly shrugged. There didn't seem to be much they could do, and Jeffrey certainly wasn't wrong.

"What do you want?" Katherine finally asked.

An extra bead of sweat formed above Jeffrey's eyebrows. He licked his lips, and a glint of yellow-stained teeth shone through.

"Well, I've surmised that you're here to overthrow Clay. Or attempt to, I suppose. So if you do end up overtaking him and his men . . ." His next blink was long, and he licked his lips again. "Somehow, I'll need your assurance that I have immunity."

"Immunity?" Katherine responded. They weren't in a court of law; there wasn't anything "official" she could give him, possibly not even her forgiveness.

"From"—he looked around the room—"everyone else."

"What do you mean?" Lee asked from behind the cuffed man.

"Ever since Clay put me in charge of a lot of tasks here, it's possible I've . . . angered people in the lower levels."

"You've angered people?" Katherine prodded. *No shit.*

"Well, there wasn't exactly protocol to be followed in this

situation, so I had to make guidelines, and let's just say those guidelines were heavily influenced by Clay because who am I to stand up to him? I have to assume the people that must follow these new protocols are not the least bit happy." He sighed. "If those people are set free, or escape, they'll be looking to take their anger and resentment out on someone, and I strongly suspect that someone would be me. It's ironic," he continued, "that I never realized this before, but it's significantly easier to follow protocol than to create it."

"Wouldn't the people go after Clay?" Ayla asked, ignoring his ramblings of protocol.

Jeffrey laughed. "Clay will go down with this ship, and nobody is going after a dead man."

"Jeffrey," Katherine said. "I can't *protect* you." She looked around to the rest of the group. "*We* can't protect you. So I'm not sure what you want."

"A group that's made it this far must have some kind of power, some kind of connection. I'm sure of it. There's got to be a way, just some assurance."

"I can see what we can do, but the only way I can know what's available for you is for you to help us in the first place." She took another step forward, and his stale breath became even more apparent. "You understand that, don't you?"

Jeffrey nodded.

"So where's the portal?"

"It's limited," Jeffrey said. "And it's code-based."

Katherine gave the signal to release Jeffrey from his cuffs. He was cornered and her team had weapons. She wasn't nearly as concerned as she used to be. Jeffrey walked over to the tipped-over desk and leaned down to look at what was once the top. He fiddled with something until a noise came from somewhere beyond the desk. A faint whine turned into an abrupt shriek, and Katherine jumped backward. The wall next to her had spun to life. What had once been a bookshelf was now disintegrating and revealing a small, two-foot-by-two-foot screen.

"Everyone, get down," Jeffrey said. "You need to stay out of view." He limped over to the monitor and stood in front of it.

Katherine fell to the floor and stayed as low as she could get. There was a bright white flash from the monitor, now obscured almost entirely by Jeffrey.

Jeffrey spoke again. "Is Clay available?"

A low, cold voice came from the monitor. Katherine didn't recognize it. "He's not currently available, but you can wait for him if you'd like."

Jeffrey nodded. "That will be fine."

"Passcode?" the voice asked.

Jeffrey lowered his voice. "Seven. Four. Six. Five. Alpha One. Uniform Nine. Romeo One. Alpha Four."

"One moment," the voice said.

Katherine twisted her body to try and catch a glimpse of the person on-screen. She could only see half of a face as it looked off the side of the screen before turning back and being obstructed by Jeffrey.

"Okay," the voice said. There was a clicking sound. The image on the screen disappeared, and part of the wall next to the monitor started to vanish, like sugar in water. The wall, now fully gone, revealed a dark red jelly-like substance. The screen turned off and Jeffrey faced the group.

"This is it," he said. "This will take you to Clay."

Derek stood, cuffs in hand, and slapped them across Jeffrey's wrists. "Thanks," Derek said. "But we can't have you roaming around free now."

Katherine took a deep breath and stepped into the portal.

TWELVE

Ellen's Confrontation

Ellen had become all too familiar with the walk to Room A, the room that once was a cordial place run by the General and had since been overtaken by Ms. Ware and who the hell knew else. She wasn't expecting anything good to come from this last-minute meeting about the orb, but she didn't have the option to decline Ms. Ware's invitations. She stopped briefly in front of the door to compose herself by looking at the floor and taking a deep breath. The doors opened and she waltzed into the room. When she looked up, it felt like she had been flattened by an invisible wrecking ball. She gasped and fell to her knees.

Clay was staring right at her. "What, Ellen, surprised to see me?" He smiled.

"What the hell is *he* doing here?" she asked after catching her breath.

"I invited him." Ms. Ware might as well have been invisible to Ellen but stood statuesque next to Clay.

Ellen wobbled to the table, and her trembling hands rested against it. Clay approached her and she instinctively took a step back.

"I know we didn't exactly part on good terms, but I'm a reasonable guy, Ellen," Clay said, twirling a knife in his hand.

Ellen backed up again. Ms. Ware caught Clay's attention. "We need her," she stated.

Clay laughed out loud. "I don't *need* anybody. She should be lucky I didn't slit her throat when she walked in here." Spittle flew from his mouth. "She tried to fuckin' kill me!" The guards surrounding the room shuffled in place. "Ms. Ware, darling, I'd like to remind you of exactly what happened so you can better understand."

"I fully understand."

Clay shot back, "I don't think you do."

Ellen didn't remember Clay picking fights with everyone, but maybe that was his new mode of operation.

"You see, my once highly regarded lead here betrayed me and helped enemies escape. Enemies that I had cornered, until she"—he jammed his knife toward Ellen—"shot at me and my guards." He twirled his knife and spun it in his hand. "The problem for Ellen here is that we have hundreds of other scientists just as capable as her, and she happens to be a known traitor."

"She's the best, and you know that. We need this to happen quickly."

"The fact that you are choosing to work with her makes me very concerned." He stopped and stared directly at Ms. Ware. "We don't *need* her help," Clay insisted. "And I should have gotten rid of her a long time ago."

"How else will this work?" Ms. Ware begged. "Communication intra-facilities will be much smoother. Can you imagine the chaos otherwise?"

"I don't care!" Clay stomped his foot on the ground. "We'll just drop in on the facilities at a coordinated time. It'll be fine."

Ellen sniffled during the pause in the conversation, and Ms. Ware turned her way.

"We have to at least see what she was able to come up with."

"Frankly," Clay said, "once again, I do not care." His full attention turned back toward Ellen. "You have exactly until tomorrow to finish. Otherwise . . ." He trailed off and dragged his knife over his throat.

"One day is impossible," Ellen argued. She knew what Clay was doing. He was setting her up for failure to have a free pass to destroy her. She was hoping her pleas would catch some empathetic part of Ms. Ware.

"Again," Clay said. "Don't care."

Ms. Ware stood stoically in the background. Ellen was not getting through to her, so she had to think of other appeals.

"It'd be easier with my team back in Kansas City."

Clay just laughed.

"What's so funny?" she asked.

"What, you hadn't heard?"

Her eyes bounced between Clay and Ms. Ware.

"Thanks to Ms. Ware here and the Colonel, your friends walked right into a trap. My men were waiting for them, and while most of them will be killed, a few will likely be spared and shoved into the lower levels like the rest of them. They'll work and crank away until they're whittled down to nothing and then discarded. But at that point, who cares? We will," he said, looking at Ms. Ware, "have come out on top, and it's no longer my problem." He took a step closer to Ellen. "So unless you want to join them, you'll do everything we ask, including making the orbs that I've requested."

It was a lot to take in, but not worth the energy to argue with the man in control of her life. She cleared her throat. "But my team is still there, yes?"

"That makes no difference to your situation," Clay spat.

"No, I just—"

"You don't *just* anything, Ellen. You're lucky you're alive."

"You said that already."

"What did you say?"

Ms. Ware stepped up and held Clay back as he continued his threats. "You had better remember your position here, Ellen. If you play nice and help, I may have a change of heart and give you a prison room with a window, or maybe just an arm through the pit instead of your entire body. I've given you everything in life, and I can just as easily take it away."

Ellen gulped. She still needed to make it safely back to the lab and get the hell out of here through her secret portal; it was even more urgent now that Clay was hanging around the place. "Getting them working in one day will take a miracle."

"Well, I guess you had better get back to work." Clay smirked.

"That's still not going to change physics." She nervously watched Clay.

"You are out of options, Ellen. You either get this done or you do not," Ms. Ware said, motioning toward Clay, whose eyes had widened.

"That's fine," Ellen said. "The General and the others will find their way back anyway. And when they do . . . Let's just say I wouldn't want to be in your position."

Clay let out a hearty laugh. "Oh, Ellen. So naive," he said, stepping forward and wiping tears from his eyes. "Your friends have already been captured and"—he looked at his watch to exaggerate his point—"the Colonel's probably already killed them by now." He had a fake sad look on his face and shook his head. "Such a shame."

Ellen had suspected as much but wanted as much information as possible before venturing outside of Chicago.

"So, what, you're just going to kill everyone in Kansas City? Is that the plan? That's a lousy plan, even for you, Clay."

His tone changed suddenly. "No. My plan is to work everyone to the bone to reach the pinnacle of power." He inched forward, his maniacal eyes lit up. "Get this working, or you'll get to experience the pit firsthand. Don't make me regret sparing your life."

* * *

Ellen practically ran back to the lab, throwing open the doors and launching the protective sheet off her secret portal. She pulled up a chair and jumped right into adding the final touches. With Clay roaming around Chicago and threatening her life, she only became more emboldened to escape this place. With the twist of a screwdriver here, adjustments of software configurations, and tweaks of the wiring, her two-way portal was nearly complete. The only question remaining now was where she would go. While once her top prospect, with the newfound information from Clay, Kansas City was probably the worst place to head off to. Unfortunately for

Ellen, that was the area she was most familiar with, and jumping back into the line of fire and intentionally choosing a place that was fully under Clay's regime seemed less than ideal.

She slammed her fists into the table. The portal shook. A small electrical component rolled off and bounced onto the floor. The portal in her office, gone. The portal in the supply room, gone. Any of the portals in her lab, gone. The options were dwindling, and she wasn't sure how to move forward, so she threw herself into her work and hoped for the best. After her portal was as finished as it could be, she spent some time fiddling with the orb. While the timeline she had been given was impossible, she was still intrigued by the engineering details. She dove deep into very technical inner workings, and as the afternoon turned into evening, according to the small clock on the wall, she realized she had made progress and gotten at least some of it working. Her fingers ached and her back muscles were twitching from spending so much time hunkered over the small ball. She finally decided to set the orb aside. She stood and stretched in the small space.

It was seemingly all one big waste of time since there wasn't another portal to escape to, but she didn't know what else to do. She pulled back on her fingers, stretching her wrists. She rocked side to side, trying to get the knots out of her back and stretching her hips. Her eyes jumped between the orb and the portal as she pondered how to proceed. She could have gone back to her room, but the pillow was probably still drying from all of her tears. It wasn't a moment she wanted to relive. It was an out-of-control moment, when she temporarily let her emotions overcome her. She preferred the electronics in front of her: stable and predictable, a problem left to be solved. But then her mind wandered to Sam and why he was one of the triggers of her emotional outburst. She didn't like to admit it, but she had relied on him. Whether for company, support, or some other reason, she wasn't sure. But what she was sure of was that he would know what to do in a moment like this. He would take in all the information and lay out options for Ellen. He was a bit of a sounding board in those moments, and Ellen started to feel things again. Regret over how she treated him. Pain over how callous she had been. An image flashed in her mind. It was Sam, in the command center, after he had been handed a weapon as his only means of protection against the unknown threat outside. Right before she entered the portal for Chicago, she remembered seeing his face. Squinted eyes. A red nose. Puffy eyes. He had been crying, and Ellen had abandoned him. She had left for Chicago to save herself, throwing him into a death sentence.

Her self-wallowing came to a complete halt as the image stayed frozen in her mind.

She left Sam.

To go to Chicago.

In a portal.

A portal she could use.

Of course. She slapped her forehead figuratively. Somewhere, somehow, Sam was laughing. He had helped Ellen once again. She stretched once more and dove into the finishing touches to direct her secret portal to send her to the command center.

THIRTEEN

Locomotion

Ayla stepped out of the portal and into a dark room. She bumped into someone. Her head splintered in pain. She was dazed, fumbling around in the darkness. She spun in a circle, looking for light. She clasped her forehead in her palms. She ran into someone else.

"Ugh," another voice said. It sounded like Lee.

A bright blue blast of light snapped the dark room, and Derek held up his illuminated weapon. "Where is he?"

"Jeffrey?" Katherine called out.

A moment passed while Derek was swinging his gun around until another voice called out. "I haven't gone anywhere," Jeffrey said in the distance. "I'm right here."

The blue light sprinted in his direction and knocked him to the ground. Jeffrey groaned as the sound of Derek's fist landed against his gut. Ayla rushed over and pulled her boyfriend off the handcuffed prisoner.

"Stop!" she shouted. The blue light only illuminated the faces of Derek and Jeffrey. Jeffrey was in pain, kneeling. "It's okay," she said.

A low humming arose from somewhere unseen, and a dim strip of lights running along the ceiling came to life. The room lit up in a basking glow.

"This is *definitely* not the supply room," Katherine said.

The room was no bigger than Ayla's apartment, with mirrors on each wall, except one wall that contained an oversized sliding door. There were two nondescript doors, one of which must have been the one they had come through. Ayla looked around, still managing her headache and trying to get her bearings, when a scuffle broke out next to her. Derek had jumped on top of Jeffrey and was taking shots with his fists. Lee and Thomas were trying to peel him off.

"Traitor!" Derek yelled.

"Cool off, Derek. Take a breath." Lee took Derek by the shoulders and walked him over to the opposite end of the room, mimicking the breathing he was trying to get Derek to perform.

Ayla jogged over to Jeffrey and extended her hand. He took it and stood. With his hands clasped together, he pressed them against his face. A large bruise was already starting to form around his eye.

"There must have been a mistake," Jeffrey said. "This is a holding cell."

"Are you sure it was a mistake, Jeffrey?" Katherine nudged him in the shoulder. "Are you sure you didn't lead us here on purpose?"

Jeffrey threw his handcuffed wrists in the air. "Why the hell would I do that? We had a deal, remember?"

"Not the first time you've actively betrayed me," Katherine remarked.

"Regardless," Ayla stepped in. "Let's just get out of here and head to wherever we need to be." She shot Katherine a look. Katherine seemed like an entirely different person than the first time they met, and Ayla would choose the old version any day, which was saying a lot since, back then, she thought Katherine was trying to kill her.

Ayla strode over to the metal door and hit a button next to it. She tapped her toes, crossed her arms, and waited.

Nothing happened.

She waited another minute, and when nothing happened, she pounded her fist against the wall.

"What'd you do?" Derek yelled at Jeffrey from the corner, Lee still trying to coach him through breathing exercises.

"Nothing, I swear."

Derek joined Ayla at the door. He banged his fists and kicked his feet and smashed the button the exact same way as Ayla had before, and still nothing happened. He groaned and walked over to the closest mirror. With little hesitation, he took aim and fired. Most of the mirror disintegrated, leaving little behind except the concrete wall it was mounted on.

"Derek . . ." Ayla reached out for him, but he was already on his way to the next mirror. He shot that one, too, with the same result. The group was starting to huddle close together in the middle of the room. They were all onlookers as Derek casually walked to the last mirror and shot it, too. Behind that mirror was still more concrete.

"Ahhh . . ." Derek yelled out. "I do *not* want to be trapped here."

"Babe, it's okay. We'll—"

"It's not okay," he said. "I've been here before."

Ayla looked at the room with a new perspective. This was where Clay must have held him captive and tortured him. Suddenly, his outburst and falling off the deep end made sense. She ran over to him and threw her arms over his shoulders. "I'm so sorry," she said. He collapsed in her arms.

"Okay . . ." Lee said. "I'm not one hundred percent sure what's happening here, but we have to figure out how to get out of here." He walked toward the only wall Derek hadn't blasted, the wall with the giant rolling door.

"Don't—" Derek reached out, but Ayla held him back.

Lee froze. His eyes nearly bugged out of his head. "Okay . . ." he stammered.

"There's a pit behind there."

Lee slowly tiptoed away.

"It's awful," Derek said. "That's how Clay crushed my hand." He held up his now-fine, cast-free hand to emphasize the point. "He slammed my hand in the door, nearly ruined it. I can only imagine what he would have done if he wanted me dead . . ." His attention fell to the floor.

"So you're saying we're trapped in here?" Katherine asked.

"Katherine," Ayla prodded, looking for a more sympathetic comment.

"I don't know," Derek said. "Ask him." He pointed to Jeffrey slouching in the corner by the door.

Jeffrey shrugged. "I genuinely can't say what's happening here."

"Bullshit," Thomas said from the middle of the room, standing near Katherine. He had been so quiet that Ayla almost forgot he was with them. She hadn't seen a spurt of energy from him in a long time, as if they were traveling with a ghost. "I've seen what you're capable of," Thomas continued. "Hell, you were leading the charge in the hospital, torturing us, running experiments . . ."

"Thomas, look, I was just doing what Clay was asking me to do. You think I wanted to be in this role?"

"Sure seems like it," Katherine said. "You were quick to turn on me and turn me in."

"Those circumstances were entirely different, you have to understand," Jeffrey pleaded. "This whole thing has not been my intention."

"What has been your intention?" Ayla asked. "You've seemed pretty sly this whole time, and how you managed to get in the good graces of Clay right when things go down . . . Awfully suspicious."

"Right place, right time, I guess. I really don't know. I promise. I have no incentive to lie to you."

"Why'd you bring us down here?" Ayla pressed. "Why not take us to the supply room?"

"I told you," Jeffrey yammered. "I don't know why we're here—" He was about to say something else but was cut off by a loud thud.

Ayla jumped as one of the nondescript doors slid open.

* * *

Mr. Fixer's boots crashed against the floor.

"We have to go." His gun was bigger than Derek's, and he crammed it against Jeffrey's face. "But you stay here," he growled. He motioned to the rest of the group. "Come on."

Ayla wasn't sure what to think anymore, but that seemed to be a theme. It was almost as if her life was on repeat now, looping through the same song. Maybe not the exact same song, but she had heard all the same rhythms and beats before.

She was trapped in the hospital, locked to her bed with all hope lost.

She got saved by Thomas.

She was trapped again at the treehouse, wanting to save her boyfriend.

She saved herself.

She was trapped by Clay in the central square, thinking she or Derek would die.

She was saved by Ellen and Shirley.

She was trapped in a tent by the treehouse earlier today.

She was saved by Mr. Fixer and Raymond.

Now, when she was trapped once more, the large man had shown up to save her again.

The record of her life had stopped spinning and seemed to be stuck in place, but once again, she didn't seem to have a choice. Between almost certainly dying, being stranded in some sort of interrogation room, or following Mr. Fixer back through the portal he had come through, it seemed like an easy choice. She grasped Derek's arm and ran straight through. On the other side, Ayla tripped over an unseen item, and only Derek's grip against her forearm prevented her from falling.

"I know this place, too," Derek said. "They brought me out here before taking me upstairs."

"Where does it go?" Ayla asked. Pain slammed into her head

again, and she grasped Derek. She held on to him until the pain had mostly subsided.

"Still having those?"

Ayla took a deep breath. "Sometimes." She was hoping it wasn't something serious and started to consider them to be stress- or trauma-induced. If she kept telling herself that, she hoped it would mean that nothing was seriously wrong with her. The thought of escaping and getting answers at a proper hospital kept her moving.

"There was another hallway . . . I think. We ended up at the elevator."

Thomas appeared in the hallway. "Where are we?"

"Sub-floor," Mr. Fixer said.

"I thought we were going to the supply room?" Katherine asked.

"Clay had his men changed portal entry and exit points now that he has access to two-way portals," Mr. Fixer stated. "We confirmed with a few maintenance workers on the lower levels."

Clever, Ayla thought.

"The General and his remaining troops are fending off Clay's men but won't be able to hold them off forever." Mr. Fixer's voice boomed throughout the small space.

Ayla clung to Derek's vest, not wanting to get lost again in the madness of the situation.

"Assuming they've got a strong point somewhere," Derek said, "maybe Clay and his team are having a hard time breaking through."

"Where, exactly, are we going?" Katherine asked from the back of the pack.

"Yeah, I don't like this," Thomas added.

"I think we've already been here," Lee said. "With Ellen?"

"Is this where we tried to get out the first time?" Katherine asked.

There *was* an odd familiarity about this place. As they approached a bigger opening and the orange lights faded, Ayla remembered trudging through trash only to get cornered and realize that what they thought was their only exit had been sealed off. It was Ellen's original emergency exit plan, the one she risked her life for, standing up to Clay and, somewhat out of the blue, helping Ayla and everyone else escape.

They had come full circle.

"Raymond was able to trace this exit," Mr. Fixer said.

"But how'd he know about it?" Katherine asked. "I thought only Ellen knew."

Mr. Fixer simply shrugged. "Everyone else is already there, chipping away at the wall, trying to find the exit."

At a fork in the hallway, they went right. The space eventually opened up to the "shrinking hallway" Ayla remembered more distinctly. As the walls crept inward on them, the group plowed forward against the rats' nest of tubes and pipes and wires. They were closing in on a light, like a welder's torch, in the distance. Mr. Fixer, being in the front of the line, occasionally blocked it out with his wide shoulders. As they got closer, a faint group of people appeared to form around the light.

"Daniel?" Lee said. The light stopped, and the hallway was only lit by dim bulbs again.

"Lee!" Daniel set down some device and awkwardly threw his

arms around Lee. "Thomas!" He did the same to Thomas. "I never thought I'd see you two again."

"I thought the same thing," Lee said. "I hear we're trying to get out of here."

"We are trying." Daniel picked the device back up. "I have to get back to it."

Raymond appeared from the shadows. "We don't have much time."

"That's what we hear," Katherine said. "I'm glad you made it out safely, though."

"For now," Raymond said. "It was more difficult than expected, but luckily, Clay has not prioritized his troops here just yet."

"What's he waiting for?" Derek asked.

"We think he assumed whatever trap he set for you in the treehouse would take care of things." Raymond kept talking. "So either he doesn't know those troops were overpowered or he is waiting for some reason. If the news hasn't gotten to him yet, it soon will."

"What's the plan now?"

Raymond shifted his attention to Ayla. "We escape," he said plainly.

Ayla rolled her eyes. "Yes, that always seems to be the case. But where?"

Raymond shrugged. "I don't know. But we can't stay here. The General is holding off Clay's men at the moment, but eventually, more men will appear, so we don't exactly have the luxury of options. It's simply a matter of time at this point."

Ayla nodded. "And how do we know the other side of this escape plan is any better? What if it goes right to Clay?"

Raymond shrugged again. "We're flying a bit blind."

"Wait," Katherine said. "How did you know we were here in the first place? We told you we'd meet up in Chicago."

"Lee," Raymond said, then gestured to Mr. Fixer. Mr. Fixer reached into the front pouch of his overalls and pulled out a small, glowing green orb.

"Oh yeah," Lee said, pulling out a matching blue one from his pocket. He smacked himself in the forehead. "Duh."

"It was just a very good coincidence we were heading this direction anyway." Raymond checked on the work Daniel was doing. "We were able to free quite a few people in the home and maintenance levels." He paused and looked around at some of the unfamiliar faces that were crouched around Daniel and squeezed into the space. "But we retreated down here hoping the supply room could be an escape route. But unfortunately, they had already damaged it beyond repair."

"Clay's portal? To get back outside?" Katherine asked.

"Yes," Raymond replied. "He likely didn't want anyone escaping, and that was the only one he knew about. So we pivoted to this long-forgotten exit, which"—Raymond held up a pair of crossed fingers—"by all calculations, was just covered up and forgotten about."

Something Clay *didn't* know about; it was as if they'd been gifted some sort of miracle that would let them get the upper hand. *Finally*, Ayla thought.

"I can't believe we didn't think to try more when we were originally down here," Katherine added, staring at Daniel as he tried to work through the wall.

"Yeah, we just kind of . . . stopped?" Lee said.

“We just didn’t have time, remember?” Ayla said. It was true that they were in a bit of a hurry, what with Clay chasing after them, but they seemed to give up so easily. They ran into a wall and assumed there was nothing else. She was surprised they hadn’t thought about breaking through the wall, but when she looked back now, they had no tools, no time, and no backup plan.

“I think we’re good!” Daniel called out. He stepped back, away from the dark spot in the wall he had been encircling with his torch.

One of the burly soldiers stepped up, having exchanged the weapon in his hand for a sledgehammer. The soldier wound up and smashed the spot squarely in the middle. Ayla grasped at her ears as the sound reverberated off the walls. With a few swings, the wall started crumbling away.

* * *

As the wall fell away, more and more light shined through the cracks. It started as a purple-yellow hue, as if shining through stained glass, until Ayla saw gemstones embedded in a large, circular steel plate. The purple faded into a dark blue, and the yellow transformed into green as more gemstones revealed themselves. In the middle of the circular plate was a spinning wheel with five teeth jutting out of the edges, like an old wheel on a pirate ship. As red and orange gems appeared, the word “AURA” was revealed, carved into the top, surrounded by even smaller, white jewels. Ayla expected something larger, like a bank vault in charge of protecting valuable assets, but as the man with the hammer stepped away, the plate revealed itself to be no larger than a manhole cover. She leaned in and saw a rectangular slot in the middle, like an ATM reader.

Raymond stepped forward. “Okay,” he said. “Everyone back.” He waddled to the circular plate and inspected it. He and Daniel exchanged whispers.

“Can I remind you,” Lee said, fidgeting with his beard from the back of the group, “that we don’t have a lot of time here?”

“Shh.” Raymond was intensely focused on something at the door, and Ayla had to guess it was the rectangular slot. She had seen similar slots before, like when she was locked in the hospital and the nurse who let her escape used a keycard for a variety of different things. She wondered if this was the same, but then again, if this had been around since the beginning of the facility, she doubted it would require the newer technology that was employed now.

Ayla clasped down on Derek’s arm as a sloshing, squishing sound came from behind the group. Mr. Fixer and Derek both turned their weapons toward the sound, and a few of the guards that had been surrounding Raymond ran forward and down the tunnel.

“Wait,” a faint voice called out from the distance.

All eyes and weapons were waiting on the man to show himself from out of the shadows.

“It’s me,” the voice said again.

Katherine stepped in front of the soldiers and held up her hands. “It’s the General.”

“Thank you,” he shouted. He took a deep breath before continuing. “We have to go. A handful of troops are lagging behind me.” His hands hit his hips and he sucked air through his teeth.

"I told them I'd catch up to you so we could wait, but our hold has been breached . . . mostly."

"Where is everyone else?" Derek said.

"Raymond, we have to wait for everyone," Lee said, but his comment went unnoticed as both Raymond and Derek kept prodding away at the wall.

"They're right behind me, but we have to go now," the General said.

"But we're still working on this door," Thomas said.

There was a loud clunking sound, like a metal plate falling off a wall.

When Ayla turned her attention back to the men at the panel, Raymond had taken a step back and was grasping at the wheel in the middle.

"It seems to be stuck," he said, grunting through a strenuous effort to turn the wheel. Daniel stepped up and pushed as Raymond pulled. Derek handed Ayla his gun and ran over, joining the men in trying to release the wheel. Mr. Fixer lumbered over and joined as well. As all four men groaned to turn the wheel, it started to inch clockwise. With each click of an internal gear, it seemed to move faster and faster.

Gunfire could be heard in the distance. The General corralled the group, moving them closer to the circular plate.

The men nearly lost their balance as the plate completed an entire rotation and sank into the wall, further and further back, until they were forced to let go. Ayla squinted as the plate slid off to the side, leaving behind only a hole no larger than the wheel.

“Come on,” Raymond yelled.

Katherine squeezed her legs through the hole, followed by Lee and Thomas. Loud noises and gunfire increased, and Ayla briefly glanced back but was unable to see anything other than a few flashes of light here and there.

“Go,” the General said.

“I’ll stay back with the General,” Derek said, seizing his weapon out of Ayla’s hands.

“You will not,” Ayla insisted.

Derek grabbed her arm and spun her around. “You need to be in there with the rest of the group. I will help the General save however many men we can, and then we’ll be through. It won’t be more than thirty seconds.”

Ayla heard a groan and looked over to see Raymond maneuvering his way through the exposed opening in the wall. She looked back at Derek.

“Hurry,” she said, reluctantly.

Derek loosened his grip and Ayla ran toward the hole. She threw one leg over and looked back at her boyfriend talking to the General. He lowered his visor, acknowledged Ayla, and ran toward the gunfire. Ayla, straddling the wall, lowered her head and went through. On the other side, the rest of the group was huddled together. She jogged over to them and Katherine stepped aside to let her in.

“What is it?” she asked, walking up to the group.

There, in front of the group, was an enormous, steam-powered locomotive. The brass and steel glinted from the dim overhead lights, and it looked like it was covered in grease. It was a giant beast, sitting in silence for a hundred years, patiently waiting until it was let loose. Today was that day. Trailing behind the powerful engine were six large wagons, like the kind Ayla played with as a kid, but each was the size of a boxcar.

"A train?" she asked.

Katherine replied, "Daniel's on the other side trying to figure out if he can get it up and running." A few bangs and clangs rang out from the other side of the train.

"This is our escape?" Ayla asked.

"This was the founders' original exit plan, apparently, yes," Katherine said.

"Where's Derek?" Lee asked.

"He's helping get people out, with the General, but we don't have long." Ayla ran to the front of the train. She found Daniel and Raymond throwing what looked like green wooden logs into an already stoked fire.

"I don't know much about trains," Raymond said, "but these . . . sticks, I guess, are getting it up and running pretty quickly. I think we're almost ready to go."

Ayla realized Raymond had lived in an entirely underground world his whole life and perhaps didn't have the vocabulary to describe logs, or branches, or trees, but she didn't have time to dwell on it. "We have to wait," she said. "Derek and the General are still back there."

"We can't wait anymore," Raymond insisted. He brushed grime off his hands and soiled his coat before walking around to the front of the engine.

Ayla followed him. "Didn't you hear? Derek and the General

and the troops are still out there." She pointed vaguely in the direction they had come from.

"This is why I never tried to get involved. Don't you see that if we don't leave, we'll *all* be dead?" A stern look ran across his face before he turned his attention to the rest of the group. "Everyone, choose a seat. We're leaving."

The smoke in the tunnel had started to build, and Ayla had to pull her shirt over her nose to keep from choking.

"This . . . doesn't seem right," she choked out on her way to the first wagon behind the engine.

Raymond wrapped a scarf around his head. "Once we get moving, it won't be so bad," he shouted through his new accessory.

She raised her voice above the engine noises and said through her shirt, "We can't leave without everyone else!"

Raymond ignored her and Daniel addressed the group. "We're going to start moving here in minutes whether or not anyone else comes through that hole."

Ayla inched toward the edge of her seat and rocked forward but was caught by Katherine's grip. She simply shook her head. Ayla knew she was right. If she jumped out to check on Derek, there was a chance she wouldn't make it back. She couldn't simply look and check; she'd have to go further back down the tunnel. The thick, black smoke rolled out through the opening. Surely Derek and the General could see that something was happening over here. She managed to convince herself they'd pop their heads through that small manhole anytime now.

The train made more noise and lurched forward.

The smoke was so thick Ayla wondered if anyone would be able to find the train even if they found their way back to the bejeweled entrance.

“Thirty seconds,” Raymond bellowed out.

As the S finished rolling off his tongue, an old, wrinkled, but intimidating face popped out of the entrance.

“Wait,” the General shouted.

“We can’t,” Raymond barked back.

The General shimmied his way through the opening and ran to the first wagon. Just behind him, Derek’s head appeared and Ayla instinctively reached out, only to be held back again by Katherine. As the train moved forward, Derek sped up. There were others following behind him, popping into the hole and through the other side, one at a time, but the train continued picking up speed. Derek was at a full sprint and reached out for the wagon. Lee, sitting near the entrance, held out one of his gangly arms and Derek grabbed his forearm. Ayla went over to help, and they both pulled him in and sent him tumbling to the floor. Derek immediately got to his feet and started barking back at the people still piling through the opening.

As the train went faster and faster, everyone who followed Derek could only make it to the second wagon, and then the third. The third wagon wasn’t even full yet and people had to choose the fourth. By the time the train was at full speed, a few stragglers were able to reach the last wagon on the line. Ayla could barely make out anyone through the smoke, which continued to build up, but there were a few who made the last wagon. She turned her attention to Derek and they hugged before she shouted out to Raymond.

“Where are we going?”

“Like I said”—he nodded—“I have no idea.”

* * *

They had either reached the end of the line or run out of fuel, Ayla wasn't sure, but the train slowly came to a halt. Everyone pulled their shirts or their hats or pieces of fabric back down from their faces, revealing mostly unscathed features compared to the rest of their bodies, which were covered in sweat and soot. Derek had let Ayla borrow his helmet, which she ripped off, letting her sweaty face finally breathe. The air was relatively cool but still warm from the smoke. Daniel stood, and his face, covered in dark-green soot and sweat, camouflaged with the surrounding cave. He was grinning, his teeth a sharp contrast against the rest of his face.

"We're here," he said.

"Where?" Raymond asked. It sounded louder than it needed to, but Ayla was still adjusting to the lack of a roaring train engine in her ears.

"I'm not sure," Daniel said.

"Ah yes, but we are *here*?" Lee chuckled. "Better than being *there*." He gripped the side of the wagon and pulled himself from his seat, quickly turning around to offer a helping hand to Thomas, who gladly accepted. Derek followed and stayed at the opening of the wagon until everyone had gotten off, then walked down the rest of the wagons, making sure everyone else had gotten off without trouble. He wrangled them all and gathered everyone next to the main engine. He stood in the middle of the circle of people surrounding him. Ayla guessed there were about thirty other people. Half were soldiers who all looked like clones of each other, and the other half were escapees from Kansas City. They were pale and either extremely malnourished or overly bulky, with little in between.

"Here's our situation," Derek said. "We don't know where we are, but we do know that this was the evacuation plan when the facility was originally built." He looked around the circle to mostly blank stares. He caught Ayla's eyes, and she could tell he didn't know the next step but had to be confident. She rested her hand against his back and he continued. "By my estimation, we've been traveling for upwards of two or three hours. Based on what I know about the geography above, we're likely in the middle of nowhere."

When Ayla first met Lee and he asked about the world outside, she imagined nondescript rural land or a secluded part of the outskirts of town. But now they were probably smack in the middle of nowhere, depending on the direction they had been traveling. With no references to go off of, it was nearly impossible to have any kind of idea.

"There is likely some kind of an exit ahead." Derek exchanged looks with Daniel, who was nodding. "There's still track in front of us, so we have to go by foot the rest of the way."

The General stepped into the circle. "And as far as my troops are concerned, members of Squad A will lead and those with B will take up the rear. New members should split up evenly in the groups. Stay on high alert. We don't know if Clay can track us here or if they're following behind."

"Right," Derek added. "I know you're tired and exhausted and probably confused, but just a little further until we're at the end." He nodded and the General returned it. "I'll lead with Squad A. Let's go."

Ayla followed behind her boyfriend.

"How are you doing?" he asked when they were about five feet ahead of the rest of the group.

"Okay, I guess."

"I know smoke always bothers you."

"Yeah, well, what am I supposed to do about it?"

Derek shrugged.

"What do you think this place is?" Ayla asked after a few more paces.

"Beats me," he said. "No idea when this was put here."

"Katherine said something about a hundred years, right?"

Derek shrugged again. "This is pretty advanced stuff for a century."

"And why it's all here, it blows my mind," Ayla added. "You think more people would know about it."

"Maybe more people do?" Derek asked. The question was rhetorical, but it snagged Ayla's curiosity again, like the first warehouse hatch they stumbled on. Maybe Clay knew, or maybe someone in their group knew more than they were letting on, but they sure weren't sharing.

"Either way," she said, "we *have* to get out of here once and for all. It just feels like we've been going round and round trying to get out with no luck."

"I know," Derek said. "I feel like a hamster in a wheel."

Ayla pondered that for a moment; that was almost exactly what she felt like, but she hadn't been able to express it.

"I wonder how Bella's doing . . ." It wasn't a question but more of a thought Ayla had stated out loud. She had lost track of time, but she knew it was way too long for her dog to be on her own.

"If we're lucky, someone realized we were gone."

Ayla sighed. "Oh, I'm sure my boss noticed but doesn't care enough to check in. Probably just fired me and gave my shifts to literally anyone else."

"I was thinking more like your brother or someone."

Ayla's life above seemed like a dream, and she tried not to think about it, but with Derek's mention of her brother, she realized at that moment there were still outstanding tasks required of her for her mother's estate, and if she wasn't there to address them, the lawyers would likely be calling her brother. He *had* to be aware that something was wrong. Ayla was suddenly extremely thankful she had given him a spare apartment key a year ago.

"Oh, I'm sure he's on it." The thought of someone even being aware that something was off gave her more hope. Things were finally starting to look up, but she knew better than to get her hopes too high, especially while they were still roaming around, entirely lost underground. She suddenly longed for her old boring life again and picked up her feet when she noticed she was starting to fall behind Derek.

* * *

Unlike how they got in this tunnel in the first place, the other end of it was nothing more than a boring dirt wall and an old, wooden door. The door was cracked and warped, barely fitting into its frame. A polished brass handle jutted outward, and Ayla was surprised that it gave way when Derek turned it. Her boyfriend inched the door open and peered past the edge. Everyone's focus was on the door. Derek held up his free hand. He mouthed the words as his fingers changed from one to two. Then he yanked the door open all the way. The soldiers behind him didn't flinch, their sights still set on where the door used to be, now a dark hole.

Ayla held her breath as the General waltzed through and crossed the dark threshold, with only the faded blue light of his weapon for guidance.

Her heart beat against her chest, ever faster as more time passed.

A lone cough echoed through the hall.

Another person sneezed.

Ayla wiped sweat off her nose.

They waited in the dark for what felt like an eternity.

Eventually, a faded orange bulb sent light through the space as the General called out, "Clear."

Derek held the door open as everyone else piled into the room. Ayla was the last, grabbing Derek's hand as she walked through. The room was at least twenty degrees cooler than the tunnel and, from Ayla's estimation, at least as big as the restaurant she worked at. The thirty people in the group fit comfortably inside and started to disperse throughout the space. It was a simple dirt floor, with accompanying dirt walls that must have been two stories high. Against the walls were rows of shelves at least half as high as the wall. The open space in the middle of the room was nothing but scattered tables with tarps and randomly assorted shelves. Ayla walked to the closest shelf, which was full of canned and jarred food and bottles and bags filled with who knew what. She picked up an old tin jar. There was a handwritten date on it: April 1912. She showed it to Derek, whose quizzical look matched her own.

"What is this place?" she whispered. A few more bulbs sprang to life as the group made it further toward the other end. The General and a few soldiers were huddled together already, seemingly hatching some kind of plan.

"It's an escape plan," Katherine said. Ayla hadn't noticed she had sidled up next to her. "This was their backup plan. They were going to send the facility here if something . . . went wrong." She kicked the dirt floor.

"Escape?" Derek asked.

"If the facility didn't work, or something like an infectious disease started spreading. I could imagine why they'd want a quick exit, so to speak," Katherine replied.

"But I thought nobody knew about it?" Ayla asked.

"*I* didn't," Katherine added. "But obviously Ellen did, and I would wager that others at the top did also."

Derek nodded. "Need to know."

Lee and Thomas walked over carrying brown bottles. Lee had twisted off the top and was in the middle of a sip as he stood next to Katherine, who immediately reached out and snatched the bottle from Lee's hand.

"What are you doing?" she asked.

Lee shrugged. "What? Tastes kind of good, actually."

"It's from 1901?" Katherine asked, examining the bottle.

Lee smacked his lips. "Whiskey, I think."

Derek asked for the bottle and threw back a mouthful. "Not horrible."

Ayla would kill for a drink, but whiskey wasn't her thing. A nice cold beer or a glass of wine would have been gone in an instant. Instead, she looked at the shelf and only found glass bottles halfway filled with murky water, more dark-brown liquid, or nothing at all.

“Derek, Ayla,” the General called out from halfway across the room.

They rushed over. The General was standing by a tall ladder leading up to the ceiling. Where the ladder met the ceiling was a simple hatch.

“This is our exit,” he continued. “We’ve searched the perimeter of the room and were unable to find anything else. We’ve sent out a small recon team, hoping they come back soon.”

“Sir—” Derek started to say.

The General cut him off. “We just need to understand what we’re dealing with. We have no idea where we are.”

Internally, Ayla rolled her eyes. *Join the club.* She had spent the last month never knowing where she was. It was starting to become the norm.

“How do you know it’s safe?” Derek pointed at the hatch. “Up there . . . wherever it goes.”

“Well,” the General replied, “when it was open, it looked like it went somewhere outside.”

“Outside . . . As in, *outside*? Not another facility or anything?” Ayla asked.

The General nodded. “Exactly. And since you’re the most familiar with the outside world”—he stepped forward—“we’re going to need your help.”

FOURTEEN

Outside

Ayla followed Derek's boots up the ladder. She flinched each time mud and dirt tumbled toward her face, but she was still convinced that him going first was a better and safer approach, given what they had been through lately. The recon team said there were no immediate threats, but being overly cautious made sense to her and Derek. As they ascended, she held her breath. When Derek reached the top and pushed the hatch door open, a cool rush of air washed over her, almost icy. Derek pulled himself up and out, disappearing behind the thick door. Ayla waited, just as they had discussed. A few heartbeats later, Derek's head came back into vision and his hand appeared through the hole.

More adventures, which once seemed few and far between, stood between her and whatever was outside this hatch.

A large, heavy sigh escaped her lungs. She was intrigued, exhausted, and wanted nothing more than to escape back to her reality. Sheer will propelled her body forward. She reached out and grabbed Derek's hand.

One breath in, one foot up.

One breath out, another rung toward the top.

Hopefully all the trauma and bad experiences were deep below and miles away now. As she got closer to the top, the tension in her shoulders and neck relaxed. She kept going up, until there were no more rungs above her. She reached the top, wrapped her arms around her chest, and peered through the biting wind, across a trace of snow covering the ground. She could see through her eyelashes just enough to notice they were in the middle of a forest. "Where are we?" she asked.

Derek shrugged. "I'm not an expert, but it doesn't really look like anywhere within a few hours' train ride of Kansas City."

The wind whipped past the couple. Derek shed his outer jacket and handed it to Ayla, who didn't hesitate to snatch the gift. She threw the coat over her shoulders and let it drape over her body.

Derek called down to the room below the hatch. "We're good. Could use a few more hands."

"What are we going to do?" Ayla asked.

"We have to find out where we are first."

"The middle of nowhere?"

"Very funny." Derek chortled. "We have to walk." Ayla followed his gaze into the distance. Light streaks of snow ran across the tops of evergreen trees and piled on fallen logs and rocks. There was no discernible path, and the only sign of humanity was the nearby hatch. There was lumbering from below, and Ayla peered in; soldiers were climbing up the ladder. They emerged, one by one, eventually followed by Mr. Fixer.

"Everyone else is staying down there," Mr. Fixer said. "For now." Goosebumps formed on his exposed forearms.

"Okay," Derek said. "Ayla, myself, and Mr. Fixer will head toward that small outcropping in the distance."

Vaguely popping out of the snow-covered ground was a beige-colored rock with a dark spot near it. Ayla was constantly impressed by Derek's training and, in this case, his eyesight.

"And the rest of you"—he turned to the three soldiers who had joined them—"head that way. We'll need to stay within sight line of each other but this way we'll cover more ground."

The soldiers nodded, formed into a tight group, and marched off. Derek turned to Mr. Fixer. "You up for this?" Mr. Fixer just nodded. The three of them staggered through a larger-than-expected pile of snow right outside the hatch and walked at their own pace toward the outcropping. Mr. Fixer quickly fell behind Derek and Ayla.

Ayla sighed. She stared off to the treetops. The hazy gray color of the sky matched her mood. Her eyes wandered down the gradient of the sky to the whites of the ground, with the occasional brown and green popping out to remind her there was still life somewhere.

"Are you okay?" Derek asked.

"I don't know anymore," she said. "I'm sorry I got us into this mess."

"Everything's okay."

She trudged through the snow. "This whole thing just isn't what I expected. It's just . . . other problems."

Derek nodded and wiped his nose but remained silent.

"I thought this could lead to a better life. I thought I'd finally be able to escape some of my past . . ."

He threw an arm around her shoulder.

"But all of my problems are still all waiting back at home for me, you know?"

"We'll work through them together."

"But it won't bring back my mother, and it won't bring my father around . . ." There was a palpable silence as their shoes crunched through the light snow. Ayla thought about everything she couldn't fix.

Her dead mother.

Her absent father.

The people in Kansas City. The children playing carefree, hiding behind their parents' legs at the pond, the little braided-hair girl in the hallway, and everyone else she had casually run into but otherwise hadn't thought about until now. Because of her actions, they were gone, probably dead, and there was nothing she could do to undo that. There was no one left in the facility to save anymore.

She dawdled through the snow, eyes fixed on the outcropping. It grew larger as they approached it.

She couldn't save everyone in Kansas City anymore, but there was hope still for the other facilities. Even though she knew almost nothing about them, she felt an intimate connection to them. It was a connection she had a hard time understanding. She had failed some but needed to keep pushing so as not to fail everyone else, too.

Mr. Fixer had fallen even further behind. He was like a toddler exploring the new world, mouth agape, eyes wide, head on a swivel. That's when it crossed her mind that he had never seen snow before. Or trees. She was amazed he hadn't passed out from the shock.

"I think maybe we've been here before." Derek's comment snapped Ayla back to the present task.

They had walked maybe a hundred yards—it was hard to tell in the snow—and a narrow dirt path appeared.

Derek jogged up to the trail and inspected it. "Fresh tire tracks."

One direction ran off to the horizon, and the other ran into a dark cave. The path was surrounded by high rock walls. Aspen trees sprouted nearby. The scent of pines hit her nose. "Wait a minute," she said. She walked to the entrance of the cave, where she paused and held her hand out. Her fingertips hit an invisible barrier and she kept pushing. She parted the empty air like a plastic curtain. Her arm jolted backward and she caught Derek's eye.

"This is the command center," she said.

* * *

"Over here!" Derek yelled out to the three soldiers a few hundred yards away. Ayla wondered if they could hear him, but Mr. Fixer must have, snapping out of his awe-inspired bewilderment and jogging their way. They waited for the surprisingly nimble man to join them at the opening of the cave.

"What is it?" he asked between heavy breaths.

"This," Ayla said. She held her hand out and parted the air. What once was a dark cave turned into a place where there was scattered light on the other end. "This is somewhere we've been before. When we escaped from Kansas City, we ended up in a . . . command center type of place." Derek nodded along as she continued. "Soon enough we found out we had to get out of there, and we walked outside only to find out it was a cave. *This* is that cave. We both remember this plastic, camouflage covering."

"Why didn't you keep going?" Mr. Fixer asked.

The memories flooded her head. The mystery troops. The guns. Being chased back in. Sam staying back. She looked around. Nothing but snow-covered trees swaying in the light breeze. "Someone was out here."

"Not anymore," Derek added.

"We have to get inside," Ayla said. Without hesitation, she pushed her way past the plastic, stringy barrier, pulling Derek along by the hand. Mr. Fixer's heavy footsteps bounced off the cave and followed them through. They ran halfway to the light in the distance before slowing their pace to a brisk walk.

"They might have eyes on this place," Derek said. "Last time we were here, we didn't stick around to see what they wanted. We ran off. That's how we ended up in Chicago."

Ayla picked up her pace, dropping Derek's hand in the process.

"What's in here?" Mr. Fixer asked, still lagging behind.

"The command center," Ayla said.

"You said that," he said. "What's different this time?"

Ayla stopped and turned to Derek. "That's a good question."

"We have troops now," Derek said. "Maybe we go back for them and hold the fort down before barreling into our next adventure?" He smirked at the word "adventure." Ayla didn't find it nearly as funny.

There was a banging near the light source at the far end of the tunnel. Ayla jumped and reached for Derek's hand again.

"Guess that changes our plan," Derek said.

The trio started running off in the opposite direction, back to the plastic tarp draped over the entrance of the cave. Ayla's heart started beating faster and the coolness of the air stung her lungs. Her arms and shoulders started to shake, as if they hadn't been used properly in years; the lack of food probably didn't help, either. She wondered if there was anything remotely edible left in the storehouse they had just come from.

The trio burst through the plastic tarp and pivoted back to the storage room they had come from. Derek lunged through the snow, trying to stay in their previous footsteps. The other soldiers were a few city blocks away, and Derek held his hand up, signaling them to go back to the hatch. Mr. Fixer and his big strides soon passed Derek and Ayla, and he had no interest in slowing down to take in the outside world at this point.

Ayla's lungs were on fire as she tried to keep up. Derek slowed to keep pace with her. "You okay?" Ayla just nodded, not wanting to use any more precious oxygen than was absolutely necessary. When she felt like her legs would fall off and her lungs would explode, they reached the hatch. It was already open, and Derek stood watch as Ayla swung her numb legs through the hole and down the ladder. Derek did the same, swinging the hatch closed behind him.

FIFTEEN

False Freedom

Ellen stumbled through the portal, tripping over herself and falling to one knee, catching the rest of her momentum with the edge of a table that happened to be nearby. She caught her breath and lowered her other knee to the ground before dropping her hand to meet it. On all fours, staring at the dirty ground, she started to cry. She had done what she set out to do. She had escaped, and the joy overcame her. She made sobbing noises like she had never heard herself make before. She had escaped Clay, overcome a chaotic situation, and was finally on her own. She was free to do whatever she needed to do. She could feel the figurative weight fall off her shoulders. After years of obeying someone, listening to someone, being under threat of someone, delivering something for someone else, it all melted away when she took one step into her secret, personal portal and away from her troubles. Away from scheming, and plotting, and planning, and manipulating.

Or so she thought.

Over the sounds of her sobbing came a man's voice.

"Put your hands in the air," the voice said.

Ellen's tears turned off instantly. Her sniffles slowed. With caution, she slowly stood, raising her hands as instructed. She was on a platform, surrounded by doors, but the man's voice had come from a lower section. As she stood and turned toward the voice, a large figure appeared at the bottom of the stairs, with a weapon pointed directly at her, along with a dozen similarly dressed soldiers.

"What I need you to do," the voice continued, "is slowly walk forward and keep your hands in the air."

Another trap, she thought.

Another calculated Clay setup.

I'm just another pawn in his game.

Events unfolded in her head and tears flowed again, but this time from failure, not joy. She held them back as best she could, but they squeezed themselves out of her eyes and down her cheek. Every time she thought she was ahead, she fell backward. Life liked to kick her when she was already down. Unfortunately, it was becoming a common occurrence. If it didn't piss her off so much, she'd shrug it off and say that's how life went. But she didn't *want* it to go that way. She wanted to be on top. She *needed* to be on top. She should be the one placing traps and outmaneuvering people. She wasn't built to be a pawn. She was meant to be the queen.

She shuffled her feet, stalling to see if she could get out of this predicament. Maybe she could bolt back through the portal, but was running back to Clay and Ms. Ware in Chicago the answer? Was it even any better?

At least they didn't point guns at me last time, she thought.

It was during her shuffling and rambling thoughts that another voice spoke up. This voice was much younger, shy, and oddly familiar.

"Ellen, is that you?" the voice asked.

Ellen's eyes darted around the commotion among the group of soldiers. From the back, someone was pushing forward. Someone emerged from the group of men. Someone familiar.

"Sam?" Instinctively, her hands rose to her mouth. Sam, once her assistant in Kansas City, had managed to help the group escape to this very command center, only to stay behind and fend off unknown attackers, allowing the group enough time to escape. Ellen vividly remembered leaving him with one gun but not nearly enough hope. She remembered feeling as though they had left him for dead. Seeing a dead man in front of her was as shocking as anything she had seen with all the recent events.

"Keep your hands up," the larger man said.

"It's okay," Sam said. He made his way past the large man in charge, who then signaled the rest to lower their weapons. Sam walked toward Ellen with his arms spread. Normally, this would make her uncomfortable, but it felt right in the moment. She hugged him.

After a few moments, she backed away. "I don't understand."

"I feel like I'm supposed to be angry with you," Sam said.

"You volunteered to stay here," Ellen said.

Sam smiled. "I know. It just seemed like that's what I was supposed to do. I think in that moment between you leaving with everyone else and before these guys broke in, I had a realization that maybe that was just how things work out sometimes. And honestly, helping the group as one of my last acts was kind of comforting. Even if I died, which I assumed was going to happen, I spent my last moments helping people live, and I was okay with that." He turned to the men behind him. "And besides, we didn't need to fear these guys anyway."

"But . . . they were coming after us," Ellen said. "You were supposed to fend them off and break the screens so they didn't know where we were."

Sam shrugged. "They came in quick and we both realized we were on the same side."

The large man who had been speaking cleared his throat. "I'm V," he said and waved at Ellen.

She waved back.

"You were with Ayla and Derek?" he asked.

"Yes," she said.

"Where are they now?"

"They're in Kansas City. At least, I think. It was a trap, so I don't know what happened to them."

"But they were safe when you were with them?"

Ellen nodded. "We were in Chicago . . ." She paused and eyed the man. "I'm sorry, who *exactly* are you?"

"These are the troops we heard trying to get in here, remember?" Sam said.

"Yes, I know," Ellen said. "But we had just escaped. You were trying to capture us again, right?"

V shook his head. "We were trying to help."

"By chasing us?" Ellen asked.

"A misunderstanding. We just needed to talk. Right, Sam?"

Sam nodded.

"But you had guns, I think . . ." After Ellen experienced a different facility, received more threats from Clay, and unwound Ms. Ware and the Colonel's relationship, her memory was all quite hazy.

"Let me take a step back," V said. "We're a security team for the facilities."

"You work for Clay?"

V made a stopping motion with his hand and shook his head. "No, no, no." He laughed. "We're external security. We work for the leadership above Clay. Our role is one hundred percent to keep people on the outside away from the facilities. Clay is internally focused only. At least . . . he has been. Anyway, long story short, we've been working on trying to rein in Clay and keep things under control."

Ellen felt her shoulder muscles relax. "And you wanted to help us because . . . ?"

"Because we need your help bringing Clay down. You're the only ones that can do it. The things Sam has told us about you are quite impressive, really."

Ellen didn't blush, but she felt like this would be a normal situation for it. She exchanged looks with Sam, who said, "You're the smartest person I know." Ellen was also the smartest person she knew, and she felt even more confident about saying that after having experienced whatever the engineering talent was in Chicago.

"Let me recap," she said. "You wanted to talk to us in this command center, about escaping and overthrowing Clay?"

V nodded. "Basically, yes."

"Why were you even here? This isn't even a facility."

"We protect the facilities and everything needed to manage them. There are quite a few roles, actually, but the important thing really is that we had been monitoring the situation when you all escaped. For various reasons, we knew you would end up here. We didn't exactly anticipate that you would be afraid of us, though, which, honestly, in hindsight, makes sense."

"Why did you ask about Ayla and Derek, specifically? Why are they so important? They're not even part of the facilities. You know that, right?"

"Look," V said, a bit annoyed. "It's not important that you know the details, but it *is* important to let us know where they are."

Ellen, in turn, was annoyed, and taken aback. To her, it *was* important to know the details. Life was all about the details, so glossing over them was both stupid and, in this case, dangerous. What if the details were the difference between life and death for her? In this case, they very much were, since on one hand she had Clay and on the other she had this unknown V character.

She gritted her teeth. "I already told you, they went back to Kansas City and that's all I know."

"Do you know *anything* else?"

"They managed to escape once. I'm sure they can do it again."

"So they could come back here?" V asked.

"That won't be happening," Ellen said. "Since I hijacked that Kansas City portal"—she pointed back to where she had stumbled out of—"I kind of figured nobody would be using that one anymore, given what Clay told me."

"What did Clay tell you?"

Her smile faded. "That he had set up a trap and everyone in Kansas City was probably all dead or enslaved."

V's tone turned serious. "That would have been helpful information earlier."

"Is that why you're here?" Ellen asked. "Because you thought they'd come back?"

V's expression didn't change. He picked up what looked like a slab of steel from a nearby table and threw it against the wall.

SIXTEEN

A Father's Touch

Ayla, Derek, Mr. Fixer, and the other soldiers stood near the bottom of the ladder. Katherine and Lee swarmed Mr. Fixer and peppered him with questions.

"What's it like?"

"Is it as magical and fantastical as our treehouse was?"

Someone wrapped a blanket around Ayla. Thomas shoved a white and gray box into her face. It was labeled "biscuits."

"Remember these?" he asked.

Ayla tore open the box and popped several dry, stale biscuits in her mouth. Daniel handed her a glass bottle. She reluctantly took a swig. There was noise and chaos. Everyone wanted to know details about what was outside the hatch. Ayla had a hard time making heads or tails of the comments swirling around her. She sat cross-legged on the floor, closed her eyes, and took a deep breath.

"Everyone," Derek's voice called out. Ayla popped her eyes

open to find Derek had climbed up two rungs of the ladder and was now looking over the crowd. “Everyone,” he repeated as the noise died down. “I need your attention.” The dirt walls absorbed the last of the whispers and murmurs.

“We’ve found something—”

Before Derek could finish, whoops and hollers roared out from the crowd. Someone whistled. Derek held his hand up to quiet the crowd.

“Quiet!” the General yelled. The sounds stopped again and all eyes turned back to Derek.

“But . . . there seems to be someone else there.”

The whipping of the wind outside squealed just above the hatch.

“It’s a cave, and it leads to the command center that runs all the facilities. We can get there, but it could be dangerous.”

“What does that mean?” Lee cried out. “We can’t have any more deaths.” His head fell into his hands.

“No,” Derek assured him. “We cannot. I can’t guarantee that, but there’s a chance we’re going to have to fight whoever is in there already.”

“I can’t fight anymore,” Thomas said. Lee leaned over and squeezed his good shoulder.

“*We* can’t fight anymore. We’re all exhausted and hungry.” Katherine looked around to agreeable nods. “There’s not nearly enough food and water here, and if we run into hostile opposition, we’ll just be overpowered.”

“I don’t think we will,” Derek said. “The command center is small. It likely only has a handful of people in it. We didn’t visually confirm who was there before coming back.”

"Why not?" Lee said.

"Lee, please be quiet." Ayla looked up at him from the ground. "This is what you wanted, right? This is what has to happen."

"I didn't want it to happen this way," Lee added.

"Neither did I," Ayla snapped back.

Derek butted in. "We need to focus. Obviously, there are a lot of things going on right now, but if we don't figure out how to get to that command center, we're going to be sitting here waiting for Clay or whoever else to trap us for good."

"Then what?" Katherine asked. "We find the command center, where do we go from there? What's the point? Can't we just walk away? Why do we have to go back? We're free now."

Ayla stood and threw her blanket to the ground. "We can't just walk away," she said, stomping her foot. "We can't leave everyone in those facilities."

"Why not?" Katherine asked.

Ayla stumbled backward. Katherine's selfish pivot caught her off guard.

Ayla pressed on. "Why would we leave them there at the hands of Clay?"

"Look," Katherine said. "I've had enough of this back-and-forth with Clay, all right?" Lee stepped forward to approach Katherine, but she shoved him away. "This isn't about us versus the world anymore, Ayla. Do you get that? This is about us getting out of the situation."

Lee tried to interject again. "Katherine—"

"Enough, Lee." Her hair had fallen out of her ponytail and was now framing her bloodshot eyes. "I know everyone left in the facilities is in a terrible position. I know because I saw it, firsthand,

and I can only imagine it's worse now. But if you think I'm going to risk the rest of my life to rescue people I don't even know, you are mistaken. I can see freedom just out there." She looked up at the closed hatch. "I can practically envision the rest of my life, and you're going to tell me otherwise? You're going to say we have to stand up for the common good?" She paused and took erratic breaths. "Who's going to stand up for me, for my good? Unless I do it myself. I can't carry the weight of the world on my shoulders anymore."

Ayla was silent. Maybe she had been naive or had misread the situation. Katherine's breathing slowed, and as Lee approached her again, she fell into his chest with tears streaming down her face. Thomas walked over and comforted her.

"If anyone doesn't want to come, then so be it," Ayla finally said. "But we have a mission. A responsibility to rescue them. *I* have that responsibility, and I understand if you don't feel the same way, but I won't be able to help you once we're out in the real world, unless you help me with the rest of the facilities."

Derek jumped off his perch on the ladder and landed next to Ayla. He threw his arm over her shoulders. "I'm with Ayla." The two exchanged a look. "Always."

The General waved off Derek's remarks. "That's fine," he said. "But we'll need a guide on the outside." He scanned the group, whose faces reflected the concern dripping from his. He sighed. "We have no choice but to help you, and besides, I'd like to get back to Chicago or at least warn them of what Clay is doing." He stepped forward to stand next to Derek and Ayla. "Those of you that would like to help us at the command center, please join us by the ladder. Those that do not can form a group by the far wall." He held up a shaky finger and pointed it across the room.

The crowd didn't move for some time. People avoided eye contact with Ayla but exchanged nervous looks with each other. It was as if they were discussing telepathically what the best choice for them would be. Some feet shuffled on the dirt floor, until Daniel was the first to cross the line. "I need to see this through," he said, to Derek and Ayla. "I can help."

"Thank you, Daniel," Ayla said.

A few soldiers wandered over, gave nods of approval, and stood next to the General. Some other soldiers walked toward the shelf on the back wall. The General seemed to have a disapproving look on his face.

"Katherine," Ayla could hear Lee say, pulling away from his ex-colleague in the Kansas City facility. "I owe it to my people to help Ayla and Derek."

"No, you don't," Katherine said.

"I have to. I started this. I'm the cause of this. I can't abandon it now."

"Why not?" Katherine asked again.

He sighed. "I just can't." He kissed her forehead and walked to Ayla. Without a word, Thomas joined him at the ladder.

"Fine," Katherine said. "I see how it is." She stormed off to the far side to join the group of those going their own way.

Raymond and Mr. Fixer were the only two that remained undecided.

"Raymond?" Ayla said. "You've seen the horrors of Clay firsthand. You don't want to inflict that upon everyone, do you?"

Raymond's chest heaved up and down and the once-pristine

handkerchief in his pocket swayed in the damp, cool breeze of the room.

"I'm afraid," Raymond started saying, "that I am of no value to your group anymore."

Ayla's heart sank to the floor. Raymond was an asset they could use in overcoming Clay and his plans, and she knew Mr. Fixer would choose to side with his boss. She couldn't compute the coldness of Raymond and Katherine, having seen everything that Clay was capable of and choosing to walk away instead of extinguishing the evil he brought to the world and the pain he inflicted on others.

"You're making the wrong choice," Ayla called out.

"From your perspective," Raymond said, turning his back and walking to join Katherine and the others against the shelf. Mr. Fixer, without saying a word, exchanged a brief look with both Ayla and Derek, then followed Raymond.

* * *

The General braced himself against the ladder. "Do we have everything?"

"As much as I think we'll need," Derek said. There was an unusual quiver in his voice.

"Let's head out," the General said. He was the first up the ladder, bounding up two rungs at a time, his weapon slung over his back and swaying with each step. In an unexpectedly agile manner, he reached the top of the hatch, hoisted it upward, surveyed the land, and finally made a hand motion to everyone waiting below.

Ayla held her hands together in front of her, hoping it would help stop the shaking. The group had scavenged what was left and usable from the storehouse, including old leather backpacks and satchels, and were now strapped with their modern weapons and century-old foodstuffs. Ayla had a small satchel slung over her shoulder with an extra pair of socks and a jar of what appeared to be water. She hoped she didn't need to find out.

This was it; this was the moment they had worked toward. Everything had been building up to what happened in the next ten minutes. They weren't sure what to expect or who would be in that command center. Whether Clay popped out or the sounds they heard earlier were from mechanical oddities, they had discussed it. Their plan, ultimately, was to overpower whatever happened to be (or not to be) in the command center and take possession of the only known way of communicating and moving between facilities. They had come this far and were minutes away from being able to free everyone.

The tremors in Ayla's hands hadn't stopped but had migrated north to her arms and were working their way to her shoulders. She took a deep breath. Derek, standing next to her, looked over and grabbed at one of her shaking hands. She slipped her fingers through his. He smiled, winked, and squeezed her hand lightly before letting go and grasping the straps of his own satchel. The rest of the General's soldiers had ascended the ladder. Derek turned to Lee and Thomas.

"Are you ready?"

"I don't think I can be any more ready," Lee said. There was a giddiness to his voice. "Let's go up there." His smile grew with each syllable. Thomas, standing at his side, still leaning funnily from Clay's torture chamber hospital bed in Kansas City, forced his own smile. Ayla had a hard time understanding his position, but he seemed to follow Lee, and wherever Lee went, Thomas was not far behind. He didn't say as much but held his hand out as if to say to Lee, *Lead the way*. Still clutching his whiskey/jar of unknown alcohol, Lee swung his arm through a ladder rung and headed upward. Thomas followed shortly after, leaving only Derek and Ayla at the bottom.

"Ladies first." Derek half bowed and let Ayla in front of him.

"Thank you, kind sir." Everything recently had been so serious and heavy that she almost forgot what it was like to joke around. It helped ease the shaking, and as she reached out for the ladder, she realized it had stopped almost entirely. She took another deep breath and started climbing upward.

Ayla reached the top and stepped back onto the snowy ground. The General and his troops had formed a semicircle around the open hatch, and Lee and Thomas stood in the middle, staring at the sky, shielding their eyes from the brightness. At one point Lee crouched down and ran the back of his hand against the snow. Without hesitation, like a child without boundaries, he fell onto his back and started rolling around. Ayla ignored him and turned her attention to Derek, who was slamming the hatch shut. It closed with a dull thud. She hadn't noticed the hatch before, but it was round, and engraved on top was a circle with three rings. She leaned in to inspect it. She traced her fingers around the rings. Inside of the rings was a small number five, and in the very center was the word "AURA." It was nearly identical to what she had found inside that warehouse in Kansas City.

"Derek—"

"I know." He leaned in. "I wonder what it all means."

"It's all connected," she said.

"Maybe we'll figure it out, but right now we can't waste any time." He stood and extended his hand. He helped pull up Ayla and then addressed the group.

"Just over there," he called out, pointing to the outcropping where the command center was. "Head toward that beige-looking rock." He marched past Lee still swirling around on the ground.

"Come on," Ayla said, following him but pausing briefly to grab Lee's hand.

"This is amazing," Lee said, stumbling back up to his feet. His eyes were glazed as if he was processing the world for the first time, which Ayla realized he technically was. Thomas was in a similar state of shock.

"We have to keep up," she reminded them.

The group trudged the same path as before, sometimes even stepping in their own footprints on the way to the outcropping. When they finally reached the sheer, curtain-like opening, Derek paused and waited for the group.

"Now," he said, "we have a bottleneck here at the top, and when we proceed through this curtain, the cave will change slightly."

"What do you mean?" Lee asked.

"This is essentially advanced camouflage. What we're looking at now isn't actually what's in here."

"You mean, this isn't a cave?" Lee asked.

"It is," Derek said. "But . . . well . . . just watch." He reached out, and when his hand hit the barrier, a line shot up to the top of the cave, revealing a crack. As he moved his hand to the side, it became wider and wider, revealing what Ayla could still only describe as a crystal-clear curtain. Hints and whispers of light were exposed in the cracks. Derek brought his hand back to his chest. "Do you see?"

Lee's tongue was practically hanging out of his mouth, and the rest of the group was stone-faced, staring ahead at where the crack once was; it had since snapped back into place as if nothing had happened. Ayla still had a hard time comprehending it even after seeing it in person multiple times. It was the best camouflage she had ever seen and never would have believed it if she hadn't experienced it firsthand.

"So, as I was saying, when we proceed—"

Derek's voice was cut off by a clanging noise near the top of the cave. Immediately, all troops focused their weapons on the unknown sound. Seconds after the noise, reality started to fold in on itself near the top of the cave, slowly falling and melting downward, and it took a few moments for Ayla's brain to comprehend what was happening. If the camouflage guarding this cave was a curtain, that curtain had suddenly become disconnected at the top and was falling to the ground. It was like they were underneath a giant, see-through flag, bending and waving as it slowly fell and folded over itself. Everyone jumped backward and bumped into each other as they tried to get out of the way. The curtain crashed to the ground like a folded towel thrown onto the carpet. Once the curtain rested on the ground, the waves and creases started to disappear, and soon enough, it looked as though nothing was there.

A bright light and a voice came from the cave.

"I thought you would never show up."

Throughout all the distraction of a heavy curtain nearly crushing them, no one had thought to check the cave. The once-dim lights were now on full blast, and a dark-skinned man was standing between the group and the entrance to the command center. Two people flanked him, dressed in all gray with a splash of green near the shoulders. All weapons immediately trained themselves on the three new figures in the cave, but the General was quick to hold his hand out. "Hold fire!" he shouted. Ayla now realized all three men in the cave were unarmed.

The man in the middle took a few steps forward. "Thank you," he said. He turned his attention to Ayla, and goosebumps burst up and down her body. Her hands started shaking again, and the longer he stared at her without saying anything, the more intense the shaking became. "It's nice to finally meet you," the man said. He took another step forward. "I believe you've been looking for me." He smiled and took yet another step forward. He was within spitting distance and he slowly raised his hand up to his waist. Ayla didn't break eye contact with him but could hear the troops around her shuffling.

The man took one last step forward and Ayla could smell cinnamon on his breath. He was only a few inches taller than her, and his eyes struck her as being very familiar, like a long-lost friend that you always knew you would recognize when you saw them again. The creases around his mouth carved deep into his tired face, and gray hairs were peeking out from the edges of his receding hairline.

She squinted.

She had seen this man before but couldn't quite pinpoint the moment.

She ran through every job she had ever had, every apartment, every ex-boyfriend, every friend and their father, until it hit her.

Her mind raced back to her mother's funeral. Mrs. Rodriguez had brought her husband, or at least who Ayla thought was her husband at the time. She didn't talk to anyone that day, but she remembered him, standing there, with the rest of the crowd. She distinctly remembered everyone who attended her mother's funeral, and he was there that day. She was sure of it.

"I've been waiting for you as long as you've been waiting for me. I've always been here, but I couldn't let you know that."

His extended hand turned into an offering for a handshake, and his smile grew even wider, further exaggerating the creases on his face.

"I'm your father," he said.

* * *

Ayla's brain became foggy. All the light in the cave washed away to a hazy gray, and a small, pinpoint of brightness remained on the face standing in front of her.

The face of her father.

The face of a man that abandoned her and her mother.

A face she imagined much differently.

His kind eyes stared at her, indicating he had some kind of soul, a soul she realized was connected to hers.

This was a moment in her life that she never thought she'd experience. A moment she had dreamed about, but he was always a blurry, faceless figure in her mind. She remembered when her mother would take her and her brother to Kansas City for a big trip, usually a birthday. She would always stare out the window, hoping to somehow recognize a face on the street and realize her father was just away temporarily in the big city. Thinking back now, she never knew how she'd recognize the face—she just imagined that she would—and now, with that face staring at her, she realized she was right. She couldn't explain it, and it made no logical sense, but she instinctively knew the face in front of her was related to her. It *was* her father; there *was* a connection.

The pinpoint circle of light started to expand, revealing more and more of his face. A stinging coolness hit her cheeks, rolled down to her chin, and bounced off her chest before landing on the floor. One tear after another until it was all she could do to hold them back. She started bawling.

The man shuffled forward and touched Ayla's shoulder. Ayla could feel Derek's hand jam tighter into the small of her back, but she pushed against him and he obliged in silence. The man put his other hand on Ayla's other shoulder and gave it a light squeeze. The man, her father, moved closer, the cinnamon still clinging to his breath. His arms lightly pulled her in closer. They embraced, and Ayla fell right into him, like a missing puzzle piece sliding right in at the end to complete the entire picture. She started audibly wailing, and the man, her father, moved his hand up to the back of her neck.

* * *

Ayla's brain was a jumbled mess. The world around her faded. Light became dark. Noise became silence. At some point, she had been helped inside the command center.

Someone put her into a chair. She sat.

A glass of water appeared in her hand. She drank.

Her father said some words. Derek said more. The General spoke. Discussions swirled close by.

She thought she saw Ellen in the distance. She was a blur.

Everyone sat in a circle. Her father was next to her, leaning forward, hands clasped.

The world became a bit clearer.

Her ears perked up. She caught her father staring at her.

"I'm sorry," he said. "I can't stop watching you."

Derek squeezed Ayla's shoulder. "So tell me," he said, "where have you been?"

Ayla's father leaned back. "I've always been here. Well, not *here* in the command center, but *here*, working for the Aura Operation."

"The Aura Operation?" Derek asked.

"That's what this *is*," Ayla's father emphasized. "That's what these facilities are. That's what these people are." He glanced at everyone else sitting nearby. "No offense," he added.

"So you're in charge of this, then?" Derek replied.

"Not exactly." He motioned to the men sitting beside him. "My team and I are more of an outside counsel, if you will."

"For what?" Derek asked.

"For the people that *are* in charge."

The General stood. "You work for Clay?"

Ayla's father surrendered his hands. "No. Clay oversees security for all of the facilities, and we oversee outside security. We work with leadership, but we operate separately. We clean up any loose ends, make sure nothing gets out. We keep the above-ground world blissfully unaware of the facilities below."

"Why?" Ayla asked, breaking free of her foggy mind. The sips of water were helping. "Why would you keep people down here, locked away, abandoned from the outside world?"

"It's complicated—"

"No," Ayla interrupted. "It's not. You let people go. You let people live their lives. You let them see how free they can be. You have to show up for them because nobody else will." She leaned into Derek's shoulders, shielding her face from the group.

"I know you're upset, Ayla. I know how upset you are."

"You have no idea," she mumbled through muffled cries.

"This is hard for me, too. You think I *wanted* to leave you and your mother behind?"

Ayla assumed this would be a better conversation to have in private, outside of this room of mostly strangers, but she would take whatever she could get. She sniffed and took a deep breath.

"So why *did* you?"

"I had to. I had to leave to protect you."

Her face was warm. "How is totally abandoning us protecting us?"

"Because of *this* place," he said. "Because if I had stayed with you, your lives would have been put at risk, and I couldn't do that."

"What do you mean?" Her head was swirling back into the deep end. It was hard to keep one train of thought longer than a few seconds.

"I've always been part of the Aura Operation, Ayla. I've always been working for them, in one way or another."

"You might have to take a step back for us," Derek said. He panned around the circle. "I think I can safely say we all have no idea what you're talking about."

Ayla's father sighed, stood, and paced inside the circle. Ayla's face had turned from warm to cold. Goosebumps reemerged, and she was on the verge of shaking. Sounds in the room seemed dampened, and the lights dimmed again.

"Okay," he said. "I will try to keep this as short as possible." He took a deep breath and sighed before continuing. "When I was twenty, which now seems like a lifetime ago, I got an amazing job offer from the government. Pay was great. Benefits were great. Everything about it was great. I was finally on my way to a stable career and your mother and I were getting established."

Most of his words were directed at Ayla, which she was fine with. After years of wondering and searching and questioning, she finally caught a glimpse of the man she had wondered about for so long. He spoke with his hands, passionate about every word. If she looked close enough, she could see her brother in his eyes. She had no doubt this was the man she had been looking for.

"A few years into that job, everything around me collapsed. The work was top secret, so your mother and I already never talked about it, but the government shut down our program, which put me in a difficult spot. I couldn't just tell your mom I had lost my job. Luckily, I was afforded a few months to find something, but the problem was, especially where we lived, there wasn't much available. Anything I was qualified for had a hard time with my so-called mysterious past job because they couldn't find anything out about it. What I thought was once the perfect job had now sabotaged the rest of my life."

He paused. The group was hanging on to his every word, so he continued. "We were still struggling to make ends meet; your mother worked a few odd jobs around town, which helped, but it wasn't much. We were trying to save up for a house and a future . . . Anyway," he continued, "one day a man showed up at my house. This is after I lost the job, so he catches me leaving in the morning. Maybe he knew I had nowhere else to go . . . But he shows up and I try to make sure your mother doesn't see him, because I don't need anything raising more suspicion, you know?" He caught Ayla's eye and flashed a smile before turning his attention back to the riveted metal ground. "He comes up to me and says, 'Vernon, how would you like your old job back?' Now, keep in mind, I didn't know this man at all. He knew my name and my old job, so I'm immediately confused. He didn't even look familiar or like he belonged in the role. It was like he was trying to look inconspicuous, you know? Like a homeless man with hundred-dollar sneakers on. It was weird."

Ayla realized for the first time she hadn't even bothered to ask his name.

Vernon.

It ran around in her head until it sat somewhere in her memory. Even his name was familiar. Her own personality suddenly became clearer; this man who knew almost nobody else in the place was pouring out his life story. She cared, obviously, but did anyone else? She admitted she was on the other side of these conversations before. Oddly familiar. And while she would have preferred to have more one-on-one time with him, she soaked in the moment, squeezing Derek's hand tighter as her father kept talking.

"I couldn't pass on the offer but wasn't just going to jump in a car with the strange man. He took me out to coffee. I remember it vividly. I got a black coffee. He ordered an extra-hot Americano, which I had never heard of before. He paid and had several hundred-dollar bills peeking out of his wallet. Whether he did that on purpose or not, I don't know." He stopped pacing and looked up at the ceiling. "It was a small coffee shop. I remember that, too . . ."

Ayla's eyes never left her father's. He was long-winded, which was surprising, but familiar. She always thought she got her chattiness from her mother, but watching this man pontificate about an event that happened a long time ago and recall minutia that seemed unimportant, she wasn't so sure. It was good to know, and good to have the information, but she didn't have time to process anything, so she filed it away for later.

"He told me it was a once-in-a-lifetime opportunity, a chance to get my job back, but of course I had questions. Was it the same job? Would I be working for the government? What kind of benefits did they provide? The whole time I was rattling off these questions to him, he just stared at me, dead-eyed, with a crooked smile poking out just above his fancy coffee. When I was done asking questions and spilling concerns, he set his cup down on his saucer, which had now been stained a dark brown, and laughed. He laughed like people in movie theaters, you know? And when he was done laughing, he stopped and stared at me again. 'Is that all?' he said. I remember it very clearly. I remember thinking he didn't understand my concerns, or my situation. He didn't know what I had just been through. He probably didn't even realize my family's predicament. I was appalled. He was dismissive, but in a weird, friendly way I didn't understand. I still can't put my finger on it." He shrugged. "But for some reason I still can't figure out, I trusted him."

Ayla sighed. She was hoping to learn more about her past but was just getting impatient. In her head, she had always imagined meeting her father and having deep, long-overdue conversations with him, but after knowing him for no more than ten minutes, she wasn't even sure she wanted that anymore. She just wanted answers.

"I'm sorry," Ayla said. "But what does this have to do with our situation?" She felt everyone's gaze. "It's just been a really long time since there's been any sense of normalcy around here, and all I want to know is why you abandoned me." Ayla stood and Derek joined her.

"I didn't abandon you," Vernon said.

"It sure as shit seems like it to me. You took this new job, for whatever reason, and just left."

"I did it to save you," he said.

"In what world is you leaving equivalent to saving me?"

"I did it to save you. This man, who I later found out was Richard, had taken over the government operation I had been a part of. It was privatized and he was running it. He was the top dog. He seemed innocent, and friendly, right?" Vernon leaned over to be at Ayla's eye level. "But the reason I remember that coffee talk so vividly . . . is because he threatened to kill you and your brother and mother if I didn't accept."

"What?" Ayla heard the word come out of her mouth, but she didn't remember asking it.

Vernon took a step toward Ayla. "I didn't have any other choice. What was I supposed to do? I had to accept. This man casually threatened my family over a coffee chat. I had to take him seriously. I didn't know what to do. I joined and he said that I couldn't ever be in touch with my family again. I tried." He looked back down at the floor. "But he was always there, watching me. I was at your mother's funeral." He gazed up at Ayla. "But he was watching. I tried to send money but he'd intercept it. He has a million resources working around the clock that I can't even begin to fathom. So what was I supposed to do?"

"I don't understand," Derek said. "Why are you here now?"

"Because I can be."

Ayla was somewhat in shock still because of the news, and now that she wanted her father to elaborate, he was simply staring at the group, waiting for someone to ask a follow-up question. "What?" she asked again, realizing that was probably her motto going forward until told otherwise.

"The reason Richard had so much power over me was because of these facilities. *They* kept me locked here, not Richard. If the facilities were gone or exposed, he wouldn't have his power and I'd be a free man, so I set a plan in place to do just that."

Ayla looked around at the group. She could hear Lee's toes clicking together because of the silence from everyone else. They all seemed as stunned as her and couldn't process what they were hearing.

Vernon kept talking, this time unprompted. "I know you, Ayla. I've watched from a distance but I know who you are. You have a constant longing for adventure, like you did as a child. You have an unexplainable empathy for people. Like your mother. You've been looking for *me* and that's always left a void in your heart." He turned his attention to Derek. "And you," he said, "are perfect for her. You provide her the protection I never could. I look at you and I see a little of myself, but mostly the drive to protect Ayla and give her a better life. It's what I've always wanted for her."

The words "thank you" fell out of Derek's mouth.

"I knew," Vernon kept talking, "that if I got you to find these facilities, you'd lead the charge in helping them escape. It was the perfect combination of adventure and empathy. If you found them, you couldn't just leave them there. You saw the conditions. You see them today. You can't *not* do something about it, right? So I just pushed you in this direction." He started pacing again. "Was it a risk? Absolutely. But everything I knew, and know, about you two said this was the risk to take. With a little help from the inside, you were the perfect ingredients to make it all work. It was this or forever be apart, which, to me, was a bigger risk." His smile grew as he took a step closer. "Do you remember the night you found the hatch in that abandoned building, back in Kansas City?"

Ayla squinted. It was a night she'd never forget, but one that left her confused. "How do you know about that?"

"The guard who was chasing you . . ." His eyes flashed between Ayla and Derek. "His outfit probably looked similar to mine, didn't it?" He pulled at his shoulder, flashing the green splash of color. "Why do you think the entrance was so easy to find? It's almost like he led you right there . . ."

Ayla shook her head in disbelief. They had ducked inside to escape the man with the gun chasing them. She remembered the distinct crunching of gravel beneath the mysterious man's feet. She had snapped a picture of him. The distinct splash of green stuck in her memory. He wore a utility belt, similar to the one her father had on.

"And the door. Didn't you ever think it was odd that it was open? And the hatch so easy to find?" Her father's eyes lit up with excitement like he had brought home a surprise puppy on Christmas morning. "I brought you here," he said.

* * *

Ayla's insides were a twisted chunk of metal.

The worst experience of her life was all orchestrated by the man she had been looking for her entire life.

Her father had sent her into this downward spiral of an adventure.

All she wanted to do was run away and pretend like this had never happened.

She wanted to bolt for the door and keep running until she reached their small, comfortable apartment.

She wanted nothing more than to run away again.

All this time she had hoped her father would bring peace and at least *some* sense of closure, but the reality was that he just raised more questions and doubts. She was grateful that he would sacrifice his own life for hers but spiteful that he'd pulled her into this nightmare. She was confused, like driving the wrong way down a one-way street in the middle of the night, when a pair of headlights suddenly popped up in front of your car. She thought she was headed the right way. She thought she had reached a place in her life where this wasn't an issue. She couldn't imagine a different ending, but the one she pictured always ended with her having a whole family again, not with her father scaring her down mysterious pathways on selfish avenues.

The entirety of her discovery of these facilities felt similar, but she was always in such a dire situation that she tried to push it down and keep it locked away. Whether she was strapped to a bed and almost drowning in goo, unable to escape from maniacal hospitals, or rounded up and nearly thrown into an unknown nether region of the world through some dark black portal, in the back of her mind, she always felt like she had vertigo, standing over the edge of a tall cliff and looking down, unable to see the bottom when the bottom started spinning. She had a brief moment of relaxation when they were safe in Chicago and she got to be with Derek again, but that didn't last long. Now, whirling through the edges of a crazy galaxy, trying to keep her balance, she thought she had finally found a space to rest, a space to recover, but she was thrown another curveball. A curveball from her father, no less.

Derek grabbed her arms, leaned in, and quietly asked if she was okay. She remembered nodding, but nothing else. The world seemed like it was both on pause and speeding by at the same time. She tried to get her bearings, but everything she did made it worse. Her mind was swimming. Her vision fading. A high-pitched buzz rang through her ears.

She tried taking a deep breath, in through her nose and out through her mouth, like her mother had taught her. She closed her eyes but the tremble of her hands distracted her. Derek's voice grew distant and mumbled. She slowly started to lie down toward his lap, and he guided her to the bench, throwing a blanket over her after she was fully laid out. He shoved something, his jacket maybe, under her head as a makeshift pillow. She focused on breathing, in and out, while the rest of the world started to fade away.

SEVENTEEN

Taking Charge

It was when the rest of the group left that Katherine realized she was responsible for what happened next. Without the General or Derek or Ayla, she had to step up. The group that put all their trust in Katherine was huddled beneath the stairs after having collected various supplies throughout the storeroom. Katherine was sad, yes, but couldn't take on the burden of involving herself anymore with the group that wanted to stay and save everyone. Although she knew there were other facilities out there, with those left from Kansas City and a few stragglers from Chicago standing with her, a strong group of twenty, she had done everything she could. She had been backstabbed by Jeffrey twice, and she didn't have the strength to dive back into the fight with Clay. After years of providing guidance and counseling to those struggling with their own health, if she didn't prioritize herself, she wouldn't be able to help anyone.

She had tried to convince herself that maybe she'd come back in the near future, and the thought of it kept her conscience at bay. She even used the excuse that *someone* had to be outside of the facilities, just in case. And *if* the worst happened, she convinced herself, and the others in the group, they'd be willing to come back and help.

She wasn't sure she believed it.

"I appreciate you all being on board," Katherine said. "But to be entirely transparent, we're all going to have to figure it out as we go." Groans and grumbles arose from the group and Katherine quickly cut them off. "I *do* have a plan, but it's a larger plan. We'll head out of here and start our own community. If we need to, we'll help others. Others who come from a trapped past or an abusive situation. Others like us."

"But we don't know how to do that," Raymond said. Mr. Fixer nodded along next to him.

"Raymond, we'll be able to figure it out. You *know* we'll be able to figure it out, right? If we can maneuver all the shit we just went through, this shouldn't be an issue."

Raymond hesitated, looking at the downtrodden faces around him. Katherine saw it, too. Those who had stayed behind were already losing hope and they weren't even out of the storeroom yet. She had to act fast. She grabbed one of the rungs of the ladder.

"Let's head out," she said, climbing hand over hand toward the hatch at the ceiling. She reached the top and pushed the hatch open with conviction. If her words couldn't convince anyone, surely her actions could. She jumped up and landed on the snow-covered ground. She had heard and read about snow, but seeing it in person was something else. Cold to the touch, it melted in her hand, reminding her of sugar, a luxury she hadn't had in quite some time. She inhaled the fresh air; the coolness of it smacked her lungs and made her rethink the whole ordeal. She quite literally had no idea about the world around her, aside from the tidbits she gleaned through books or from the passed-down stories from the original elders of the facility. She noticed footprints heading off into the distance where the other group had traveled. Not wanting to interfere with their plans, she focused in the opposite direction.

The sky was a surprising gray color. She was used to either the pitch dark of the underground or strong beams of light coming from the Mirror in the central square; there wasn't much in between. She let her mind wander and she thought about snow falling and what the experience must be like: white dots of coolness peppering the sky and landing quietly on the ones before them. She wondered what it was like during other times, or if it was always snowing. Green trees popped up from the ground and were a stark contrast against the grayness of everything else. It was beautiful. She could have stopped here and stared at the beauty for days, but her attention was drawn to Raymond stumbling to the ground. She lent him a hand as he scrambled to all fours and carefully stood, dusting snow off his singed and smoky blazer.

"Fascinating," he said.

"Exactly," Katherine replied, staring up at the sky and focusing on the trees in the distance.

Mr. Fixer tumbled through the hatch shortly after Raymond but didn't say much about their new surroundings. The three of them—Katherine, Raymond, and Mr. Fixer—remained silent, staring off into the distance as the rest of the group climbed out and found their footing on the unfamiliar terrain.

This environment was so different from the world below that Katherine wondered why Clay would go to such an extent to hide this from everyone. Why would *anyone* want to hide this? She knew the answer was power, because that was always the answer; she saw that with Ellen, she saw that with Jeffrey, and she saw that with Clay. Watching the group climb out of the storeroom and into their new world, she hoped the power wouldn't get her, too. She liked to think she'd be different than other leaders, and she hoped that Raymond or Mr. Fixer would keep her in check if that happened, but this was unknown territory, and part of her felt like tossing any and all experience aside to start anew.

"This is where we start fresh," she said. "This is where we leave our old lives behind and build new ones." Some group members were still gawking in the distance, but most were paying attention to the speech she was making up on the fly. "I'm going to give everyone one last chance. If you would like to join the other group, their footsteps appear to be tracking that direction." Katherine pointed off into the distance. "I don't know if our trek will be easy, but I know it will be easier than anything we've encountered so far. We have experience and knowledge and the capability to build ourselves a new life, and to help others." She paused to take a deep breath. She had the attention of everyone around her, and she felt like she was once again atop the Beacon, giving direction from above. It was uplifting. She started to believe that they *could* actually do this. "If you're with me, let's go." She stepped forward and parted the group, heading in the opposite direction from Ayla's group.

She didn't know where she was going.

RISING ABOVE

She didn't know what was in store for her when she got there.
All she knew was that it was better than the alternative.
All she knew was that she could make it, no matter the obstacle.

EIGHTEEN

A Daughter's Thoughts

"Ayla . . ."

Someone was gently rocking her body.

She opened her eyes.

It was Derek.

She smiled. Tucked in under a warm blanket, with her boyfriend by her side, like back at home. Maybe it was a weekend and she had slept in. Derek had already taken Bella for a walk and made breakfast in their tiny kitchen. They'd sit on the couch and watch some stupid show while sipping coffee and talking about all the fun stuff they'd be able to do one day. When she closed her eyes, she could practically smell coffee and burnt-just-right toast, and she was in her happy place. Away from her need to escape, away from her desire to find an adventure. She was exactly where she wanted to be.

Mysterious strawberry jelly walls left her mind and were replaced with strawberry pancakes.

Being chased by guards was washed out by her and Derek running through the park.

Memories of Shirley and the other helpless victims were replaced by vivid memories of visits to her mom in hospice care.

Before her mind could turn dark on her, she opened her eyes.

Had it all been a dream?

Was it a vivid Alice in Wonderland nightmare?

She blinked and looked past Derek. There were other strangers milling around, inside the all-too-familiar command center. She sat up and threw her arms around her boyfriend.

"You okay?" he asked.

"I'm fine." She pulled away. "Thank you for being here for me. It's been . . ."

"I know." He smiled. "Remember when you just *had* to go back to that stupid hatch?"

She smirked. "Didn't know it would turn into such a big ordeal."

"Nothing major. Just running from psychopaths, being held captive, meeting your father of all people . . ."

Ayla's smile turned into a laugh. It was an absurd reminder about humor. They were still in a huge pile of a mess, but at this point, she wanted her old life back and whatever it would take to do that. She had spent so much effort trying to run away and realized where it had landed her: absurdity she didn't care for. Even her father wasn't the man she thought he'd be, and she wasn't sure where to rank "getting to know this semi-stranger" on the list of current priorities. At the top, though, was just getting back to her old, boring, predictable life. She still had a strong desire to save whoever was trapped below, but now she realized it might not be worth the cost of her own sanity.

"We'll be home soon," Derek said.

Ayla smiled. "Are you sure about that?" She had thought the same thing many different times, only to end up somewhere completely unexpected. She appreciated her boyfriend's optimism.

"Well, that's the hope. Here." He stood and extended his hand to help her up. "We scrounged up breakfast. It's not pancakes, but it's not terrible."

"Let me guess. Stale crackers and water?"

Derek just smiled and led her to a makeshift buffet, which consisted of some food plopped down on a cleared-off counter against one of the walls. Others in the group were huddled and heaping portions of the feast onto their makeshift plateware. She spotted Ellen in the distance and rubbed her eyes to make sure. Next to Ellen was also someone familiar.

"Ellen?" She stepped toward her. "And... Sam?" she blurted out.

Sam turned and smiled.

"Ayla," he said.

"I thought—" Ayla started.

"Yeah," Sam interrupted. "So did everybody, but as it turns out, your father and his men were just wanting to chat." He let out a lighthearted laugh. "Who would have seen that coming, right?"

"And Ellen?" It sounded like a question but wasn't. Ayla just wasn't sure what else to say.

"Things went south in Chicago." Ellen set her food down on a chair next to her.

"I kind of figured," Ayla replied.

"So I had to make an emergency escape portal for myself. I'll be honest," she said. "I was a bit surprised to find out you were here, along with everyone else, but I suppose I shouldn't be. You have a way, Ayla"—she twirled her hands around in the air—"of just surviving." She paused. Ayla didn't respond, so Ellen finished her thought. "I admire that."

Ayla hadn't thought of it that way before, but especially from Ellen's perspective, that was probably true. "Thanks?" It was all she could think to say.

"Oh, no thanks is needed," Ellen said. "Just know that I'll be coming to you for any tips in the future."

Ayla put on a crooked smile. "I'd love to catch up, but maybe after I grab a bite to eat?"

Ellen and Sam both nodded and then returned to their conversation, while Ayla shuffled back to the food. She grabbed some crackers but mostly just wanted water. She had taken only one bite before her father approached her.

"How are you feeling?"

She let the question hang in the air for a while before replying. "Fine, I guess."

"I know this probably isn't what you had in mind, meeting me this way for the first time—"

"You can say that again."

"But," he continued, without missing a beat, "you have to believe me that I was doing what I thought was the right thing. For everybody. Your mom, your brother, you . . . I was trying to make it all work."

"I'm sure you were."

"I didn't think everything would be horrible in the facilities." He touched her elbow, and they locked eyes. "I'm sorry."

His eyes stung. They reminded Ayla of her mother slowly

shrinking away in hospice care. She had spent a lot of time just looking into her eyes, in a "motherly love" kind of way. She got that feeling from the man in front of her now, a "fatherly love," although she was finding it hard to admit to herself. She diverted her gaze to the floor.

"Well, it was horrible."

"I know that now, and I'm sorry. But it was something I had to set in motion to finally break free of this place. Look around. Do you think I enjoyed this either?"

"Are you comparing your journey to mine? Because at no point in your story did I hear about you almost dying and getting locked up and chased by people with guns."

Vernon didn't say anything. He apparently knew when not to say something, a trait Ayla wished she had more of. She went back to the food table and mostly shuffled around a few things.

"Can we just, I don't know, start over?"

"Maybe," she said, without turning around. "It kind of depends on what happens here."

"Look," he said, biting into a biscuit. "I know I may not have given off the best first impression."

Ayla rolled her eyes.

"And I'm sorry for that." A piece of dry biscuit clung to the side of his mouth before detaching itself and tumbling to the floor. "I did a lot of reflection over the past few hours, and I can see how you might be, let's just say, not that happy with me."

It was the understatement of the century, but Ayla didn't want to call that out. She wanted to see where he was going with this.

"I apologize that I came off that way. I think I was just maybe overly excited to finally meet you in person. I can't imagine how hard it's been for you, and putting myself in your shoes for a few hours made me realize that I probably come off as the bad guy to you."

"You're not the bad guy," Ayla interjected against her best instincts. It didn't need to be said, and she wasn't sure if it was even true, but she felt like saying it.

"I am, though, from your perspective," Vernon insisted. "But that's okay. I think I can accept that. I may have made a poor choice all those years ago, but I swear, my intentions were to protect you at all costs, and to keep you safe, and to just . . ." He looked around the room, searching for the words to help him out. "To just . . . do my best." His soft eyes fell on Ayla's.

She wanted to give him the benefit of the doubt.

She wanted to reach out and hug him and tell him it would be okay.

She wanted to, but she couldn't.

She couldn't let herself get close.

She didn't even know this man, and while he said the right things, he didn't show them.

"I'm going to need some time," she said. "To process . . . everything. Okay?" She wanted to expand and explain it all to him.

How she would have made different choices.

How he left her looking for a male role model her whole life.

How she had to raise her brother.

How she had to be strong while her mother was dying.

How this whole thing was because of him.

How she left looking for adventure because her life had been so difficult and trying and stressful that she just wanted to escape it all.

She wanted to say so many things, but instead, she walked back to Derek.

NINETEEN

Setting a Trap

Ayla was tired. She was tired of everything. Tired of deciding direction. Even though she had fought to come here and try to save the facilities, her brain was foggy and she couldn't make a big decision. She wanted to lean on others for help. In this case, the room was buzzing with energy. Derek and the General were already chatting.

"Kansas City is clear," the General said, exchanging a brief glance with Derek. "As clear as it can be."

Ayla caught her boyfriend's eyes darting to the floor. Something seemed off. "What does that mean?" she asked.

"It means there's nothing left for us to do there."

"Nothing left?" Ayla pressed.

"They're all dead," Derek said. He took one step back from his girlfriend. "We were down there," he continued, pointing at the General. "We saved who we could. The others were on their deathbeds, and with Clay's men ravaging through the lower levels, those that could escape with us are here." He looked around the room. "These *are* the people from Kansas City. And those that left with Katherine." He gestured broadly in the general direction they had come from. "Consider the Kansas City facility"—Derek stumbled for words—"out of commission."

Ayla gasped. She should have realized it sooner, but there was a lot happening. She didn't fully appreciate the moment at the time, when they left on the train. Everyone on board *was* the facility. There was nothing to go back to. "So the only people that left were those chasing you to the train? Clay's men?"

Derek nodded.

Ayla processed this for a moment. This was her goal, after all. She wanted to save the people in Kansas City. She just failed to realize there were so few left to save. And those that could be saved, in fact, had been saved already. "So what are we doing here?" she finally asked.

"The command center is all we know right now. It leads to all the other facilities," the General said.

The glow of the monitors highlighting people in the other facilities caught Ayla's eyes, and the doors with the other cities on them were standing tall in the distance. She mentally drew a red X through the door labeled "Kansas City." That was when she realized they were too late. Clay had overtaken Kansas City and what was left was standing in front of her, relatively speaking. They couldn't just go through the rest, city by city, and expect to be effective. It was like following a tornado and picking up the pieces afterward. They had to get in front of the tornado and evacuate. Or better yet, they had to destroy the tornado.

"We need to find Clay," Ayla said.

"What?" Her boyfriend's reaction mimicked the faces of everyone else.

"Clay," she replied, "is the problem. Clay is causing this, isn't he?" She looked over at Vernon.

Vernon nodded. "That's what I've been trying to say. He's a dangerous man who will not stop until he's the only one left. It hasn't always been like this, but it's getting worse."

"Then we stop him," she continued. "We find Clay and we free the facilities."

Vernon continued nodding.

"Are we . . . sure?" Lee jumped in. "I mean, as much as I love the guy, he has literal soldiers following him."

"I don't think they will follow him," the General added. "He's more like a dictator, and I expect there's little to no respect. The forces he's in charge of are simply following him at the moment, but if we can remove him from the equation, I don't expect they'll complain."

The hierarchy and relationships between Clay and his men were something Ayla didn't want to have to think about. She merely exchanged looks with Derek, who gave a slight nod of approval, and deferred judgment in that area to the man who was more familiar with it.

Ayla spoke with confidence. "I agree."

"That's all well and good," Lee said. "But how in the world do we find Clay? He could be, quite literally, anywhere."

Vernon cleared his throat. "I can actually help with that." All eyes were on him as he stepped forward. "I may have a way to get in touch with him." He held up his hand, and inside of it was a dark black rectangle: a cell phone. Ayla had spent so long underground she had forgotten all about phones and the world she left behind.

"What is that?" Lee asked.

Vernon flipped it open, revealing a keypad and a dim screen. "It's a phone."

"*Fone?*" Lee asked, looking quizzically across to Thomas, who was staring at the device in Vernon's hand.

"Oh right," Vernon said. "It's a way to communicate with someone."

"Like the orb?"

"The orb?" Vernon asked.

Lee pulled out a glowing blue orb from his pocket.

Ayla grasped at her head and then pain sent her stumbling backward. Derek caught her before she fell. "Ayla," he said, reaching out.

The room shuffled, and Ayla caught her balance in Derek's arms. "I'm fine."

"Ayla?" Ellen asked. Her voice seemed concerned.

"It's that orb." Ayla pointed toward Lee, who quickly pocketed the ball. "I've noticed it in portals, too. I get a headache when I go through them or when I'm around that thing."

"Hm," Ellen said. "Has this always happened?"

Ayla rubbed her forehead. "What do you mean?" It was odd to see Ellen care about another person.

"I mean"—Ellen stepped forward—"have you always had headaches, or is it a recent thing, with the portals and the orb?"

"It started when I got to the facility. I broke in above some room, saw one of those orbs being worked on, and then was blasted with pain." Ayla adjusted her eyes as the pain subsided.

"You . . . saw an orb being worked on?"

"I think. I don't know." Ayla held back her frustrations. She was confused as to why Ellen was so hung up on this detail.

"What were they doing, specifically?" Ellen pressed on.

"Look, I don't know, okay?" Ayla let go of Derek's arms. "We don't have time for all of this. Phone is old tech; orb is new tech. And yes, Lee, they work similarly." Her attention turned to her father. "How can you get in touch with Clay?"

He cleared his throat again. "Well, my person on the inside is someone with extremely close ties to leadership. Leadership that knows about *you*, Ayla. But they don't like intervening; that's what Clay is for."

"So they sent Clay after me? You worked with the people to send them after me?"

"No." His voice boomed throughout the center. "I'm working with one of the good guys on the inside. He wants to see the facilities fall, just as I do. But you have to understand, we can't just rush in and save the day. This has all been calculated, and so far, it's gone mostly according to plan."

Ayla scoffed. "I'd hardly call this a successful plan."

"Sure, there have been some bumps, but you're free, and Kansas City is free, right? I actually didn't plan beyond this. I wanted you safe, and I wanted to save Kansas City. I didn't realize the rest of the facilities were in danger."

"Well, you probably should have," Ayla added.

"An oversight. Fine. So kill me." He chuckled. "I'm sorry. I'm trying to make the situation a little lighter, okay?" He pinched his forehead with his fingers. “Anyway, the man I’ve been working with has direct access to Clay. I just tell him there’s been an emergency and we need help. Maybe he’ll come right to us.”

TWENTY

Steven

Clay stepped away for a bathroom break. Steven was halfway through his call list, confirming and verifying cut orders across the board, not just for food but other supplies like medical items, building and research materials, daily essentials (which was practically cut to zero), and miscellaneous items Richard had added over the years. He liked to add art and books, which he thought helped keep the residents at peace, but Clay thought otherwise. Not every supply list item made it to every facility, but most of them had their own unique extras they clung onto. With Clay, it was guaranteed that these items wouldn't make it to *any* facility.

Steven hung up on his latest supplier, dropped the phone, and let his elbows rest on Richard's old desk. Steven had worked endless hours at this familiar desk, but his recent work was different. This time, he had a gun to his head, both figuratively and literally at times. Steven rubbed his eyes and stood; the chair rolled off the wooden floor and onto one of the many rugs Richard had collected and scattered around his old home. Steven paced around it, paying more attention to the details that had escaped him so many times in the past. Richard was a man with fine taste, and even the carpets reflected that. It was a shame it would all go to waste.

His phone buzzed against the oak desk. His eyes darted to the *RESTRICTED* caller. He quizzically picked it up and held it to his ear without saying anything.

"This is V."

Steven eyed the room before lowering his head, cupping his mouth, and whispering, "I told you not to use this number."

"It's an emergency," V said.

Steven's eyes darted around the room again. "What?"

"We need Clay at the command center."

They were the words Steven had been hoping to hear for far too long. Their long-winding and sometimes convoluted plan had fallen into place. The man on the other end, the man from the external security group, the practical stranger, had helped orchestrate an undertaking Steven was almost sure would backfire. It meant the facilities were starting to topple, and the end was in sight. It meant that Clay was the lone remaining obstacle. It meant that V was ready to remove that obstacle.

"As soon as possible," Steven whispered as a dark shadow loomed in the corner of his vision.

He cleared his throat and raised his voice. "Look, there's not much I can do, okay? I have to work." The other end of the line clicked, and Steven knew V had hung up. He continued talking anyway. "What do you want me to do?" He waited a few ticks in his head before replying to the nonexistent person on the other end of the phone. "No," he exclaimed. He jerked the phone away from his ear and dramatically pushed the *End Call* button.

"Tough times at home?" Clay's voice came from behind Steven.

"Sorry, I was just taking a break."

"No, I get it," Clay said. "Family comes first, right?" His tone and demented smile felt like a trap.

"I took care of most everything. I just have a few more calls to make but I'm working my way through the list." Steven pulled the chair close and sat.

For some reason, Clay had another apple in his hand, but this time he was slicing pieces off with a knife Steven didn't know he had with him. As Clay stepped closer, Steven realized it was the knife he had used to murder Richard. Clay stepped forward, and Steven rolled backward, bumping into the table.

"What?" Clay asked, still smiling. He looked down at the knife in his hands. "Oh," he said. "*This.*" He held it up and the light from the candelabras on the wall glinted off its surface. Clay twisted and turned the blade, sending the reflections bouncing around the dimly lit room. "I just . . . you know . . . needed a knife. And I had this one on me, so . . ."

Clay took another step forward, further cornering Steven against the desk. He thought, momentarily, about trying to run, about knocking Clay over and hoping to get past him. Clay knew where he lived. He knew his information. He'd track him down in a matter of hours. He'd probably never see his wife again, and he wasn't sure if Clay would kill or torture him.

"You don't think I'd use this to hurt you," Clay said, inching forward. "Do you?" His smile flattened out and he took one more step toward Steven, collapsing the personal space bubble entirely. Steven could smell the pink lady apple on his breath. Clay raised his knife. Steven closed his eyes. He didn't know what to expect. He peeked through them just in time to see Clay plunge the knife into the apple in his other hand, now at chest level. Clay sliced off a thin piece and popped it into his mouth. "I'm just eating an apple," he said. "Get back to work." He turned around and wandered over to the fireplace, leaning against the mantle, chewing his now-tarnished apple. "When you're done, let me know. I've got some business in Chicago."

A response wasn't needed, so Steven just nodded. A bead of sweat fell down his face, and he used the rolled-up sleeve of his button-down shirt to wipe it away.

* * *

"Look, Brady, I've got a ton of calls to make today. You're not the only one hit here by the cut across the board, okay? Just cut back our order twenty-five percent for the foreseeable future." Steven was tired of these phone calls but was nearing the end of the list.

"Twenty-five!" Steven could practically hear the fear through the end of the phone line.

"I'll keep working on the bosses, but that's all I can do now."

"What about just twenty?"

"Sorry, Brady, I don't have any flexibility."

This was pretty much how all the discussions had gone today. Coming up next was the counteroffer.

"Twenty-three?"

Like clockwork, perfectly in sync with the grandfather clock ticking away in the distance. Clay hadn't gone far; he was in the dining room, cranking away at something on his laptop while Steven was plowing through the supplier list, all the while trying to figure out how to get Clay to the command center and tip over the last domino. In between the highly predictable negotiations, Steven had hatched a plot as best he could. Steven knew Clay, though, and the man wasn't likely to fall for a simple trap. The sweat dropped down and splatted against the desk. Steven dabbed at it with his sleeve again.

"It's twenty-five and there's nothing I can do about it."

After this call, he wanted to summon Clay and spring his trap. He practiced breathing exercises between calls and was at the point where he just wanted to rip off the metaphorical bandage. There was a long silence. Steven practiced more patient breathing as he waited for Brady to break the silence.

"Fine," he said. "Twenty-five. But you're killing me, Steven."

"Believe me," Steven said, "this is more painful for me than it is for you."

"Doubt it," Brady said and hung up. The phone went silent.

Steven hung up and cleared his throat. "Clay," he called out. "I need you for a minute."

Angry shuffling sounds came from the dining room. Clay appeared just over Steven's shoulder. Steven swiveled around in his chair. Clay didn't say anything.

"Something's wrong at the command center."

Clay stepped forward. He continued not saying anything.

Steven swiveled back to the computer and pulled up what was supposed to be the security feed for the command center. He had rigged it so there were now only blank screens. Predictably, Clay commandeered the keyboard and started fiddling with settings. The screens flipped over from one blank screen to another.

Clay slammed the keyboard against the desk. "What'd you do?"

Steven rolled away. "I checked it between calls. I don't know."

"Well, shit," Clay said.

"Do you want me to go check it out?" It was rare that Steven was able to visit the command center, but he wanted to offer because that seemed like something that a good employee would do. He anticipated Clay's response.

"No, you have work to do here." He dropped the keyboard again and it smacked the desk. "Don't do anything stupid while I'm gone." With those parting words, Clay marched back to the dining room, grabbed his jacket, and headed off to the portal for the command center.

Steven waited and counted to sixty to make sure his boss wasn't heading back. Then he turned off the laptop, admired Richard's impeccable taste, left through the front door, making sure to lock it behind him, and headed home.

* * *

He was hoping he was leaving Richard's house for the last time. He paused at the doorway to the garage and took in the peace and serenity of being in such an opulent home without a maniac looking over his shoulder. He wondered what would happen to the opulent place but also didn't care as much as he used to. Steven slipped into his Mercedes, weaved through the country back roads, and slid onto the highway. Instead of hopping directly into the fast lane and racing home, he stayed as far right as possible, soaking in every minute of this newfound peace.

A world without Clay.

A world without the facilities, finally.

They had consumed nearly his entire life.

Rolling down the road in quiet, Steven realized the stress that had built up over the years had simply vanished, as quickly as the passing trees outside of his window. It all seemed to melt away. Even the headlights on the opposite side of the highway seemed more peaceful than before. The brake lights went from frustrating to fascinating. The way they lit up the road and oil slicks appeared almost beautiful, in a way. Even the moon shined brighter than before, and Steven was no longer worried about much, if anything. He didn't love that Clay had unceremoniously flung Richard's body into a black, soulless pit of a portal, but as he cruised ever closer to his house, even that worry faded. He loved Richard, but if his death led to the path of a Clay-less world, and a stress-free life, he considered it a fair tradeoff. It was hard to worry about much when Steven would wake up tomorrow morning without anything on his agenda, for the first time in his life.

He rolled his Mercedes into the four-stall garage of their Victorian-era, twelve-bedroom home. He pulled up next to his wife's SUV, a toy Corvette, and an old Viper. He twisted the keys in the ignition and the engine shut down. He threw his head back on the headrest and exhaled before opening the door. He stood, stretched his legs, and let the driver-side door fall shut. The car lights faded, and as he walked past his car collection, the automated lights lit up his path to the entry door. He took one last deep breath before turning the knob and stepping up into the large mudroom.

The house was quiet, so he propped his hand against the heavy door and guided it shut, quietly clicking it into place and touching the lock button to engage the security system again. He strolled on the travertine floors, through the updated kitchen, past the seldom-used dining room, and into the reading room, where he found his wife, reading a book in the tall-back leather chair. He stepped onto the wood floors and they creaked. His wife didn't look up from her trashy romance novel. "Welcome home," she said.

He briskly walked toward her, leaned in, and kissed her forehead. "I missed you," he said.

His wife turned a page. "What do you need?"

"Nothing," Steven said. "I just love you." He sat down on the sectional sofa on the other side of the room, tossing aside one of the many decorative pillows. "How was your day?"

His wife peeked out over the book. Steven just smiled from the couch.

"What?" she asked.

"I just want to know how your day went." Steven slumped further into the couch and kicked off his shoes, sending them flying next to where the pillow had landed.

"Do you mind?" His wife dropped the book into her lap and set aside her one-of-a-kind, ornate reading glasses.

"It's fine," he said. "Don't worry."

"Excuse me?" She sat up in the chair. "I *am* worried. You seem not like yourself. Are you feeling alright?"

Steven's smile widened. "I've never been better. Thanks for

asking." Steven wanted so badly for her to know the truth, but he had worked so hard over the years to build an elaborate lie about his corporate life. Maybe someday they could talk about it, but today wasn't the day.

His wife furrowed her brow before picking up her book and putting her reading glasses back on.

Steven loved his wife, and he loved his life, more than ever.

He closed his eyes and listened to the crackling wood in the fireplace.

TWENTY-ONE

Clay

Ayla was leaning against the wall furthest away from the portals, expecting Clay at any minute. The General and his men had encircled all portals and were simply waiting to grab whoever came through whichever one.

"Are you sure you're okay with this?" Derek asked her.

"I'm okay as I'll ever be, I guess. Are *you* okay with it?" Derek had his own history with Clay. It undoubtedly had created some trauma that he would never admit, at least not for a long time. He might even take it to the grave.

"I'm fine," he said.

He wasn't ready to talk about it. Typical, but unsurprising. Once they were past this, it would be easier, but for now, Ayla would take it and was hoping it was a sign of what their lives would become again. Typical and unsurprising. She was tired and didn't want to be surprised anymore. She had worked her energy up to get through whatever happened with Clay, and then they'd figure out the rest, but at least that maniac wouldn't be threatening them at every turn. Lee seemed jovial, off with the rest of the group, chatting about the outside world with Thomas and Ellen and others from Kansas City who had never experienced it. It was like they were where Ayla was a while ago: wanting something new and exciting and not wanting to wait to discover the newfound world. Except their new world was her old world, and she was more than okay with that.

"What if he doesn't show up?" Ayla asked.

"I trust your father," Derek replied, keeping his eyes on the portals in the distance.

"Based on what?"

His attention returned to Ayla. "He's apologized several times, and his intentions are good."

"Are they?" Ayla had a hard time wrapping her mind around this practical stranger who claimed to want the best for her.

"What would he even get out of lying?"

She hadn't considered that perspective. Visions of her and her father bonding after all this craziness was over played through her head. They'd meet up with Jake. They'd take Bella on a walk and chat about Mom. They'd laugh at movies they had both seen but were watching together for the first time. They'd drive by the house Ayla grew up in. It seemed almost too good to be true, but maybe she had just been burned by recent events. Derek was right; she had no reason to think her father was lying, and it wouldn't even make sense if he was.

A commotion by the portals shattered her perfect future and reminded her of the frightening present. Derek ran off in the direction of the noise. Lee and the rest of the group scurried around, looking for cover.

Ayla froze. Clay had entered near a guard. He was fighting. The General was shouting. The rest of the guards came over. Clay tried to run back and escape. Someone dove on top of him. A pile of guards. Clay was probably on the bottom.

"No," someone shouted.

"Get up," another voice said.

"Don't shoot."

"Get up."

Some grunts. Pounding noises, clanging noises, loud thuds.

Ayla inched her foot forward. She had to convince herself to keep going. She gave herself a pep talk internally. She was so close to the end, just a bit further. She could do it. She reached the stairs to the platform and grasped the railing. One step at a time. The commotion was still happening. She was past the second step, then the third, then kept going until she was on the platform. The bustle had faded, and standing by the portal was Clay. Two guards had grabbed his arms, the others pointing their guns directly at him. Derek and the General were facing the madman, but no one was speaking. Clay's jacket was askew and falling off a shoulder, and his hair was scattered on top of his head. A few red marks smeared across his face. His knee bent awkwardly, causing him to lean against the guards.

"This is impressive," Clay spat. "I really didn't think you had it in you." His eyes darted between Ayla, Derek, Lee, and Ellen. Blood dripped from the corner of his mouth. He spat again. "How'd you do it?"

Vernon stepped forward. "I've been working with someone on the inside."

Clay cursed. "Steven," he whispered. "I should have killed him when I killed Richard." He stumbled, held up only by the guards. His shoes made squeaking sounds against the floor. "So what now? Are you just going to kill me?"

"Why shouldn't we?" the General asked. "You sabotaged us. You killed half my men. You exterminated the facility. You are a threat to everyone."

"I barely even know who you are." Clay laughed. "What the hell do you even know anyway?" He raised his voice. "None of you know. You have *no* idea. And even if you did, you don't have the guts to do what I do. You don't have it in you to lead the facilities, let alone lead other people. You don't know what it means to be a leader. To have a vision and execute." Spittle flew from his mouth, and blood dripped from his chin onto his jacket. Sweat was forming on his brow and his hair waved back and forth as he wiggled against the restraints of the guards. "You're all just jealous anyway. Jealous of what I've become, of what I *can* become, and you're angry you didn't get there first." He paused and took a breath. The room was silent. "What, nobody has anything to say? Not surprising. A bunch of weak-spined children. A dog that caught the car and now they don't know what to do."

Lee caught the General by surprise, leaping onto the platform and grabbing his gun. He aimed it straight at Clay before Derek could extend his arm and jolt the weapon upward. A shot rang out, and a blast bounced against the far cave wall. The room ducked. Clay and the guards holding him fell to the floor. Derek quickly wrestled the weapon back from Lee.

Holding his hands up to his face, Lee said, "I'm sorry. I don't know what came over me."

"Ha," Clay said. "I didn't think you had it in you, old man." He laughed. "If only you were a better marksman."

"You don't deserve it," Derek said, handing the weapon back to the General, who closely eyed Lee as he headed back to the group. "You don't deserve any respect, quite frankly. But beyond that, you deserve the pain you've put everyone else through."

"Derek—" Ayla started to say.

"He doesn't deserve anything." Derek raised his voice. "Except for the pit."

There was an audible gasp from those in the room in the know. As Ayla recalled, the pit was used as a torture device: once to threaten Derek, and then again when they pushed the Colonel into it so they could escape. The pit, as she understood, was a portal without another end attached to it. There was no consensus among those she spoke with about what happened when people went into the pit, other than they never came back. It was as fair a punishment as Ayla could come up with. Clay was far too dangerous to be left somewhere in the facilities, for fear of one of his allies coming along and freeing him. And letting him loose in the world was equally precarious, with his connections and know-how. Even then, she'd expect Clay to end up in a powerful position in a short time.

Lee shouted from the group, "As much as I love that plan, we don't have a pit here, Derek."

Ellen stepped forward. "That's not entirely true. I can make one."

"Oh great, of course," Clay spat, standing again and fully

content in the arms of the guards. "Once a promising apprentice that I had considered to help with the overthrow, and now she's standing here plotting about how to destroy me." He huffed. "You know, Ellen, you are just as pathetic as your old boss. I should have purged you back in the day, too."

"Shut up, Clay," Ellen snapped back.

"How?" Ayla said. "How would you make a pit?"

"We use what I created to get here," Ellen said. "It's a bit of a makeshift portal and should be sitting on a table in the lab in Chicago. We go back through where I came from, destroy the one I created sitting on that table, and then the portal here will be a brand-new, shiny pit awaiting Clay." The smile grew on her face.

"But doesn't that mean whoever destroys yours will be stuck back in Chicago?" Ayla asked.

"Yes," she said, looking around the group. "That is one of the downsides, I suppose."

"I'll do it," the General said without hesitation. "I need to be there anyway, for the rest of my troops, and to squash whatever it is that Ms. Ware is planning."

Ayla suppressed an instinct, an instinct to save the General. It was easier that she knew he wasn't walking into a death trap. He could fend for himself and likely even thrive. With Clay and the Colonel out of the picture, the General was as poised as anyone to help take on Ms. Ware in Chicago.

A hush fell over the crowd. There were no last-minute volunteers to step in for the General. He took a deep breath before handing his gun to Derek and addressing him and Ayla. "I appreciate everything you've done," he said. "Not just for me and my troops, but for these facilities. I trust you will do whatever is necessary from here on out." He stepped toward the portal to Kansas City: the portal Ellen had hijacked. "I assume you'll know when the other has been destroyed."

Ellen simply nodded from the edge of the platform.

"Then I'll be quick," the General said. He turned to Derek and Ayla again. "I hope our paths cross in the future." He took one more deep breath before stepping through.

* * *

"Well, that makes my life easier," Clay said. "You really just sent your best soldier, your leader, away? For some reason?" His lips flapped together. "One less person I have to defeat whenever I get rescued."

"You're not getting rescued, Clay," Derek said.

"Hey, where's Katherine anyway? Shouldn't she be here with you?"

"You don't have to answer that," Derek said to the rest of the group. "It doesn't matter."

"Ha," Clay laughed. "Trouble in paradise, huh? Even when everyone gets everything they want, I guess it's not as they expected." He smiled, and his cold eyes darted to Ayla. She felt exposed, as if he had been reading her thoughts.

"How long should this take?" Derek asked Ellen.

"Not long, unless he's having trouble destroying it. Or is having second thoughts . . ."

Ayla didn't know much about the General, except that he was fiercely loyal. In no way was he having second thoughts.

"He's not having second thoughts," Derek added. "He's a man of his word." Another man seemingly reading Ayla's mind.

"It shouldn't be particularly tough for him to destroy, so . . ." Ellen trailed off.

"Maybe he's on Ms. Ware's payroll," Clay added. "Maybe you've been betrayed yet again. God, wouldn't that be great?"

"Don't listen to him," Ayla said. "He's just playing games. He's trying to stall. He has nowhere to go." She turned to face Clay. "He's afraid." Her eyes pierced his.

"How many times have you thought that to be true?" Clay asked. His gaze broke Ayla's and panned the room. "How many times did you think you were going to get away with something only to find out that wasn't the case? Admit it, I've had the upper hand this entire time and you—"

Ellen punched Clay in the face. Blood spattered the wall behind him.

"I've been waiting to do that for years," she said, shaking her hand out.

Clay whimpered, "You hit like I'd expect."

"What?" Ellen said.

Derek held her back. "He's trying to rile you up."

"What'd you say?" Ellen pressed.

"I said," Clay started, with more energy, "you hit like I'd expect you to hit."

The portal behind Clay faded from red to black, and the edges lit up white before dimming to black.

"And what is that?" Ellen asked.

"Like a runner-up," he said. "Like someone who doesn't have the fortitude to do what needs to be done." He spat blood onto the floor, and some landed on Ellen's shoes. "Like someone who keeps telling themselves they're climbing to the top of the mountain but doesn't actually have the guts to do it. Like someone who doesn't even know what they want in life and always finds an excuse to not do it. You're pathetic," Clay said, blood dripping from his teeth. "I can't believe I ever had faith that you'd be that person. I was just lucky enough to come to my senses before it mattered. If only I had killed you before you shot at me and ruined my plans in Kansas City. It had all come together so perfectly, and the one thing I didn't plan for was you to have a change of heart and help the enemy. I should have taken you out when I had the chance."

"Yeah, well," Ellen said, "you didn't." She shoved Clay as the guards let go, and he fell backward. His torso hit the pit first. The outline of his body lit up in white as the pit engulfed it. His legs stumbled through after. The same white light lit up the outline of his legs as they fell in. The light traced his thighs, and kneecaps, and shins, until finally his shoes, spattered with blood drops, continued falling backward and into the pit. One final, bright white light emanated from the pit before it returned to its inky-black state. Ripples appeared in the blackness, like a velvet blanket smoothing itself out. When the last ripple stopped, the pit returned to a calm, blank-slate canvas of nothing but black.

TWENTY-TWO

True Freedom

Ayla had a hard time processing what had just happened. She had personally pushed the Colonel into the pit and remembered it being a surreal experience. As an observer, it seemed the same: slow and agonizing, but at the same time immeasurably abrupt. One moment, Clay was here, terrorizing the facilities, and the next, he faded into nothing. Literally nothing. He just disappeared. There was no other side to the portal; Clay was just gone.

Derek smiled and said, “We did it.” Ayla’s disappointment must have been visible. “What?” he asked.

“Clay’s gone, sure, but there are still people out there and trapped.”

Derek grabbed her shoulders. “But we’re free. We have time and flexibility to figure the rest out.”

“But Derek,” Ayla said. “I’m tired. I can’t do this anymore.

I want to help, but I just . . ." She sighed, staring into Derek's forgiving eyes. "I just can't."

Ellen cleared her throat. "Actually, I think there's something you *can* help with." Everyone's attention was focused on her, in the center of the circle.

In the commotion and reflection with Derek, Ayla had nearly forgotten that the rest of the group was here. "What?" she asked, leaning away from Derek and instinctively running her hand through her hair.

"Your headaches," Ellen continued. "That you told me about. The incident when you first arrived, with the orb? I believe they're connected. If you experience it every time you go through a portal"—she looked at Ayla to confirm, who simply nodded—"then I can't help but think that experiment you witnessed somehow connected you with the underlying technology."

Ayla scrunched her eyebrows. "I don't understand."

Ellen explained. "The portals—and the orbs, too—use essentially the same technological foundation. I'll try to keep it simple, but when you were there for that experiment, the communication channels that are used were somehow . . . ingrained in you. For better or worse, you essentially *are* another orb, at this point. Except it seems that you may be able to experience them all at once rather than point to point, like it was designed and intended for."

"So you're saying I can communicate with the orbs?"

Lee chimed in and held up a finger. "Aren't there only, like, a few in existence, though?"

Ayla nodded along.

"Orbs, yes," Ellen stated. "But because of the shared core

technology, you're also linked to the portals. You can communicate with the portals. They're like orbs for you."

"But the portals aren't used for communication."

Ellen rubbed her forehead. "Right. But without making your head spin, just know that because of the technological overlap between portals and orbs, for all intents and purposes, portals *are* orbs for you. Essentially, they use the same broadcast technology. So while portals aren't used for communication, that's true"—she nodded—"you *can* use them that way."

Ayla thought back to her time with Shirley. They were in her room. An announcement from a hidden speaker somewhere. It had played Katherine's message. It was a warning about how Clay and his men were coming for Lee and Ayla. At the time, Ayla didn't think anything of it.

"You have to understand, all the technology here is built on top of everything that came before it. From what the General was telling us, the other facilities share some technology. Surely, I imagine, at this point, they've been given portals, just for the sheer convenience of them."

Ayla's mind was spinning faster, trying to figure out what Ellen was saying, until it clicked. "So I can communicate with the other facilities?"

Ellen stopped pacing. Her eyes caught Ayla's. "I think you can, yes."

* * *

"We can test it out," Derek jumped in.

Superhuman telepathy that could also work as a broadcast

system seemed a bit bizarre. But then again, there was no normal feeling ever since she walked through the strawberry goo portal and stumbled on these facilities. It was like a dream, except this was real, and she was in control.

Derek scurried to the platform and pointed to the various screens. "We can see the other facilities." His finger darted to the screen underneath a sign that said *New York City*. "We can see them." His finger moved to the *Washington D.C.* screen. Some people wandered in and out of the frame. The monitor under *Kansas City* was eerily blank, and the one by *Chicago* showed a broad view of the main space, no room specifically. Ayla wondered if the General was already plotting how to overcome Ms. Ware now that he had sacrificed his freedom to be back there. If she could help him in some way by letting the people know, she'd jump at the chance.

"Those have to be using the same technology," Ellen said. "Otherwise, they wouldn't work out here . . . wherever we are. They have the tech. We have the means. It's perfect."

There was a pause as the room fell silent. The previous buzz of energy collapsed in on itself as all the attention and focus turned to Ayla.

"Even if I *can* broadcast something, what do I say?"

Silence still, until a mutter came from a man in the back. It was Ayla's father.

"Tell them the truth. I should have told *you* the truth a long time ago and should have never let this all happen." He stepped forward and let his hand drop onto his daughter's shoulder. "I'm sorry." A tear formed in his eye.

Tears tugged at Ayla's eyelids. She dabbed them with the back of her hand and let it come to a rest on top of her father's. "It's okay," she said. "I don't fully understand the choices you made, but I really do believe . . . I *have* to believe you were doing what you thought was best."

Vernon smiled and nodded as tears flowed down his cheek.

Ayla sniffed and then turned her attention to Lee. "You've done this before, right?"

Lee's eyes widened. He pointed at himself. "Done what?"

"I mean, you've used an orb, right? You can help me figure it out?"

Ellen interjected, "Just use it like a walkie-talkie. You have to focus on where you're communicating and then just think about what you want to say."

Lee added, "Use the screen. Focus on them. Start somewhere. It took me practice, but if anyone can do it, you can."

Ayla took a deep breath, grabbed Derek's hand, and pulled him with her as she stepped onto the platform, heading for the screens. He obliged with no hesitation. She slowly walked to the *Washington D.C.* screen. She paused and dropped Derek's hand. The people on the screen were blissfully unaware of how their lives were about to change. They were people just like everyone else. Were they happy? Were they sad? Were they frustrated or angry? Did they feel trapped or oppressed? Ever since finding out about the other facilities, she had assumed the people in them were just like the people in Kansas City: under the thumb of a ruler who didn't care about them. But seeing the people on the screen talking with each other, walking to and from places, and generally behaving normally had her second-guessing everything. Maybe she had gotten it all wrong, but maybe she was right. She glanced over her shoulder at her father, tears still drying on his cheek. He blew her a kiss and it all felt so surreal. She closed her eyes and considered what she had just been through.

A negligent father who assumed things for her.

A facility in Kansas City that made assumptions about her.

A maniacal leader who was operating as selfishly as possible.

Everyone was looking out for their own best interest. Their assumed interest. But what was missing in it all was choice. The choice Ayla never got to live with her father. The choice her mother never got to battle cancer. The choice the people of Kansas City never got, having been born into their situation. Ayla wasn't happy about how her choices had led her here in the first place, but at least it was a choice she was able to have. She wasn't locked into her life; she and Derek had made choices to get where they were. Ayla made the choice to run away and find this place. It turned out, in retrospect, she might not have made the right choice, but it was hers to make, and she got the chance to make it. It all came down to choice, and depriving people in the other facilities of their own choices was immoral. Ayla had an obligation to make them aware, to give them a choice.

She opened her eyes and took one step closer to the screen. She focused on the people, imagined what it was like there, and let her instincts take over.

Her forehead crinkled. The right side of her face started to tingle. The edges of her vision blackened. All she could see was the screen. Her ears stopped hearing everything. Noises only came from within. It was the people in Washington, D.C. Murmurs turned into conversations. Shivers formed at the base of her neck and inched upward until they crested at the crown of her skull, exploding into a shattering pain, but Ayla maintained her focus. She started to shake, like an overused muscle, and her vision went blurry until it faded entirely before erupting into a black and white image of what she had seen on screen. It was as if she could see directly what the screen could.

She took a deep breath before speaking—or, rather, *thinking*—the words. In through her nose, and out through her mouth.

"Hi," she said, not knowing how else to start. "You don't know me, but I have an important message for everyone here."

The people in her vision stopped in place and turned toward her, or wherever her voice was coming from. Slowly, more and more people came into her field of view. She kept talking.

"I don't quite know how to say this, but you're not alone. There are other facilities. You have been controlled by someone who doesn't want you to know that." She paused again, watching the people in their disbelief about what they were hearing. It reminded Ayla of when she found out her mother's cancer was terminal. Simply shock. She hoped the people would hear the rest of the message.

"However," she said, "that person is gone now, and nobody is in control." She wasn't quite sure how to finish. "You can choose to leave if you want to, or stay."

The people were reflecting on what she had just said. Ayla tried to ignore the pain that had now spread to her entire body. She tried to remember any other details.

"There's likely a way to leave the place you're in," she said, thinking back to how they got out of Kansas City. "Ask whoever is in charge, or look for a portal in a supply room somewhere. I don't know details about your facility, but that's how we got out of ours. It leads to the real world."

She felt like she had to explain herself, so she kept going, holding back exhaustion spreading throughout her body. "I just felt like you needed to know this information. I felt like you needed a choice."

She pulled away. Her legs gave out from under her, and Derek caught her in his arms.

"What'd you say?" Ellen asked.

"Ellen, please, give her a minute." Derek laid her down on the floor. Her father came running toward her with a glass of water. He held it to her lips and Ayla took a sip. Her pain subsided faster than she expected, like being eased into a hot tub and feeling all tension and soreness escape her body. She sat upright.

"What'd you say?" Ellen asked again.

Derek held out his hand. "How do you feel?"

Ayla looked around. The group was eagerly waiting to hear her response. They must not have heard what she said. Had it been in her head only? She licked her lips and smiled. "They heard me," she said.

Ellen ran to the screen. "Something is happening down there. I don't know what, but something."

"You got through to them!" Lee exclaimed.

Ayla caught Derek's eye. "I think I did." She smiled.

* * *

"I can help," Sam said. "I mean the other facilities. I can help them get out. We have access, right?" He pointed to the doors with the same city labels on them. "Now that they know, we can go and help. We can get them here."

"Or if they have a similar train to escape," Lee added.

"Or some kind of escape plan," Ellen said. "I'm sure we can find someone to help there." She turned to Sam. "Sam and I can team up on that."

Ayla stood. "Are you sure? You don't want to leave this place with us?"

"Not yet," Ellen said. "I want to make sure everyone gets out." She headed toward the screen that said *Chicago*. "And besides, I have my own personal follow-up I need to look after."

"Ayla," Derek said. "As long as you send that message to the other facilities, I'm sure Ellen and Sam can cover it."

"We can help, too," Thomas said, standing next to Lee. "Right?"

Lee nodded. "It was what I always wanted. It feels like an extension of what I was meant to do."

"Okay," Derek said. "Then that's it. That's all we need to do." He smiled. "We're almost done."

It was what Ayla had been trying to accomplish for a long time. The time was here, and it hardly felt real.

She repeated the same message to the other facilities, making sure to take rest and water breaks between each. All the facilities seemed receptive, and Sam, Ellen, Lee, and Thomas monitored the screens for activity and developed their own plans to get everyone out safely who wanted to get out.

"Thanks, Ellen," Ayla said. "I know we haven't always been on the best of terms, but we couldn't have done this without you."

"I know," Ellen said, smiling. "I thought you were a spy for the longest time. Based on what your father told me, I'm still not sure that you *aren't* a spy, just maybe an unwilling one." She laughed.

"I'm sorry if I upturned your life." It felt like the least that Ayla could say.

Ellen nodded. "You did. But I think that's okay."

They shook hands. "Good luck," Ayla said. "When you're done here, come find me."

"I can't imagine you'll be difficult to track down." Ellen held up the orb that Lee had stolen.

"Will I always have this ability?" Ayla asked.

Ellen shrugged. "I think so, but you're charting new territory, so it's hard to say."

"At least I know someone who can help if it comes to it." Ayla smiled.

"Always," Ellen said.

Ayla walked over to Lee and Thomas. "Are you sure about this?"

Lee nodded. "I've never been more sure in my life." Thomas nodded along.

"I appreciate everything you've done."

"No, Ayla," Lee added. "I appreciate everything *you've* done. We were marching down the path, but you were what we needed to finally cross the finish line."

Ayla smiled. "I'm sorry," she said, addressing Thomas's still-bandaged shoulder. "That wouldn't have happened if I hadn't come here."

"Look around," Thomas said. "None of this would have happened if you didn't come here. If this is the worst to come out of it"—he shrugged his injured shoulder—"then that's a small price to pay, isn't it?"

"I suppose so," she replied. There was a brief, awkward moment of silence before Ayla broke it. "Please find me when you're done here, whenever that is."

"We will," Lee added. "Even if I have to wrestle that orb away from Ellen." He laughed.

The three of them hugged in a weirdly shaped triangle before Ayla headed back to her boyfriend, who had been talking with Vernon.

"What now?" Derek asked.

"We go back to our lives," she said. "Our beautifully boring lives."

Acknowledgments

This book, and the entire series, is an undertaking of many. I'd like to especially thank Bodie Dykstra, a great editor who constantly polishes my words and ideas. I'd also like to thank Ben Mcleod, the talented design eye who crafted the immaculate covers. There have been several people along the way all throughout, and without them, I simply could not have done it.

Writing is often seen as independent, but every writer knows a good support system is always needed. As always, I appreciate the understanding and support from my family: Karla, Aizlynn, Emery, Friley, and Charley!

www.ingramcontent.com/pod-product-compliance
Lightning Source LLC
LaVergne TN
LVHW090935080826
845145LV00003B/760

* 9 7 8 0 9 8 4 3 0 9 6 5 8 *